"I dreamed you were going to ask me to dance," Suzy murmured.

"Dreamed it?" Kevin repeated carefully.

She blushed. "Yes." She shook her head. "I'm saying too much, aren't I? I'm embarrassing you—"

"No!" He touched her cheek. "This is the way I dreamed it too," he admitted with a rueful grin. "I knew your skin would look like gold, and be this soft and warm to the touch. I knew your hair would be a flame . . ." He stopped, narrowing his eyes as if to keep her from seeing into his soul. But then he said softly, "I'm burning anyway."

His hands wove into the spill of her hair, its color shadowed to russet by the darkness. His fingers grazed the tender nape of her neck, sending shivers of delight racing along her spine. She stood motionless beneath his touch, breathless . . . waiting.

"And I dreamed this," he told her as his fingers caressed the pale chiffon of her dress, then slipped beneath it to trace a delicate line across her heated skin. Suddenly he pushed his hands into her hair and drew her mouth up to his. She clung to him then, the kiss filling her with a cool sweetness, and she thought, *Dreams do come true . . .*

WHAT ARE *LOVESWEPT* ROMANCES?

They are stories of true romance and touching emotion. We believe those two very important ingredients are constants in our highly sensual and very believable stories in the *LOVESWEPT* line. Our goal is to give you, the reader, stories of consistently high quality that may sometimes make you laugh, sometimes make you cry, but are always fresh and creative and contain many delightful surprises within their pages.

Most romance fans read an enormous number of books. Those they truly love, they keep. Others may be traded with friends and soon forgotten. We hope that each *LOVESWEPT* romance will be a treasure—a "keeper." We will always try to publish

LOVE STORIES YOU'LL NEVER FORGET
BY AUTHORS YOU'LL ALWAYS REMEMBER

The Editors

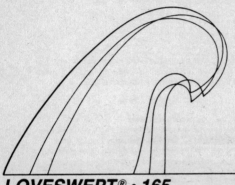

LOVESWEPT® • 165

Adrienne Staff and Sally Goldenbaum
Kevin's Story

 BANTAM BOOKS
TORONTO • NEW YORK • LONDON • SYDNEY • AUCKLAND

KEVIN'S STORY

A Bantam Book / November 1986

ISBN 0-553-21800-X

Published simultaneously in the United States and Canada

PRINTED IN THE UNITED STATES OF AMERICA

O   0 9 8 7 6 5 4 3 2 1

For our friends, with many thanks for their encouragement and support!

One

"Oooh, why does it have to be so hot?" Suzy Keller plucked at her new silk dress. "Why *today*?"

"Because it's August and it's Kansas City," her younger sister replied as she drove north on the interstate, leaving behind the big homes and fancy shops of the Country Club Plaza. "And because I can't afford to have the crack fixed in my air conditioner. Want to pitch in, sis?"

Suzy grinned. "If I get this job, Nikki, I will personally finance a new air conditioner for you. Maybe a whole new car! All you have to do is keep your fingers crossed and pray. Deal?"

"You bet. It's wonderful to have a soon-to-be-rich, soon-to-be-famous sister." Nikki changed lanes and concentrated on finding the right turn-off for the warehouse district, which was located on the banks of the Missouri River.

Suzy's nervous laughter floated out the window and disappeared on a hot, humid breeze. Soon to be famous? she repeated silently. Her? Suzy Keller? Her gaze lit on a giant billboard advertising a radio station and her heart skipped a beat. The images blurred before her eyes, then disappeared, and she saw herself up there, Suzy Keller, smiling out at the freeway drivers, enticing them to covet, not just her, but the boxes and boxes of cookies upon which she sat so alluringly.

She smiled at the vision and closed her eyes to concentrate on her appointment—and her plan of attack. Her head was a clutter of strategies and hopes, rehearsals, bits of conversation guaranteed to impress. Leaning forward, she tipped up her chin and flipped down the visor mirror. Smiling, she showed a white flash of perfect teeth and a darling dimple.

"Oh, hello, Mr. Ross," she said to her reflection. "How nice to meet you. Why, you're much younger than I expected for a man of your accomplishments." Pause. Smile. A toss of her blazing red hair.

"Good grief, sis, what are you doing?" Nikki asked, glancing over at Suzy.

"Practicing!" Suzy said, frowning.

"You don't have to practice. You're perfect!"

"Uh-uh. Christie Brinkley's perfect. Cybill Shepherd."

"You're as perfect as they are!" Nikki said, and laughed. "The world just hasn't seen as much of you yet. Besides, if you ask Mom, no one's perfect except Suzy Parker, and *you're* about to follow in her footsteps."

"Sure, Nikki. And if you ask Mom, Dad's a combination of Lee Iacocca and Paul Newman and you're Mother Theresa! Ohhh," Suzy groaned. "Maybe I should forget it, or at least wait until Lorraine comes back on Monday."

"Don't be silly, Suz! You've gone to interviews without your agent before. And as you said, if you wait, someone's liable to beat you out and become the 'one and only, sure to be famous' Kevin's Kookies girl, and you will miss this golden opportunity, this next rung up on the ladder of success, and lovely Lorraine will wring her hands, and—"

"Enough! I give! Just tell me, do I look all right?"

"Gorgeous! You'll knock his socks off!"

Suzy's mouth twitched up at the corners. "Great, and what if he has hairy feet?"

"Well, you'll soon find out, kiddo. Here's your exit."

In minutes they were parked in front of a square, squat dusty-red brick warehouse. No frills. No flashy sign. This building meant business, all business. And what about the man who owned it? What would he be like? Suzy wondered. Would he like her? Would she project the right image, match that fantasy in his head? Would he hire her?

"Go for it, sis," Nikki said. "Good luck . . . and break a leg!"

"Wrong business, but thanks anyway." Grinning, Suzy stepped out of the car, slipped her portfolio and its cache of publicity pictures from the backseat, then leaned over to her sister. " 'Bye, Nikki."

"Sure you don't want me to wait?"

"No, you go buy your water bed. I'll grab a cab to celebrate! See you later."

Moving like bright water in her silk dress, Suzy walked slowly to the front door. She hesitated there, her hand on the old wooden knob, feeling the hot sun on her shoulders and the backs of her legs. Another minute and her hair would begin to curl ever so slightly across the nape of her neck, and that wouldn't do at all. Not now.

She blew a puff of air up under her heavy bangs. Mid-August and hot in Kansas City, and hot and still here in the warehouse district, the heat shimmering off the pavement. The fish market across the street was locked, the shades drawn. But the telltale smell of salmon and swordfish, flounder, snapper, and catfish clung to the street. Nearby, the stalls in the farmers' market were empty, everyone having fled by noon. It was quiet, so quiet she could hear her own breathing, the nervous rat-a-tat-tat of her heartbeat. With bold determination Suzy squared her shoulders, knocked once for formality's sake, and pulled open the heavy wooden door.

The noise hit her like a splash of ice water in the face. Conveyor belts, motors, timers, bright yellow fork-lifts hustling boxes across the wide floor. Doors swung open and banged shut again. The ceiling, latticed with steel beams, caught all the noise and threw it right back down at her.

Suzy flinched and covered her ears with both hands. Her portfolio thumped to the floor and she let it lay there. She could feel the noise right through to her bones. How could these people work like this? she wondered, shocked.

She looked around at the bustling activity. There were people everywhere—lifting, stacking, sealing, pulling and pushing boxes of cookies. And no one at all seemed bothered by the din. No one but Suzy.

"Hello?" She tried calling, lowering one hand in a faint little wave. "Hello? Is Mr. Ross around?"

No one turned, no one waved back, no one noticed Suzy Keller at all. So much for first impressions! she thought. Retrieving her portfolio, she picked her way around a stack of unsealed cartons and over to the nearest workman.

"Hi," she said, then louder, "Hi! Excuse me, I'm looking for Mr. Ross. Sir . . . ?"

She tapped him on the shoulder and he spun toward her, knocking a carton off the conveyor belt as he turned. Forty-eight boxes of chocolate chip cookies slid across the floor.

"Oh . . . oh, no! I'm so sorry!" Suzy exclaimed,

horrified. "I—I was looking for Mr. Ross's office. I am *so* sorry!"

The man's initial anger vanished and his bushy mustache twitched as he smiled. He patted her once on the arm, winked, and pointed toward the rear of the warehouse.

By then two younger men, eyes glued to Suzy in rapt adoration, were busy picking the cookie boxes up from around her ankles. They stuffed them back into the carton, then stood there, staring at Suzy like lovesick pups.

The older man gave a short, soundless laugh and sent the two boys back to their jobs with a quick jerk of his thumb. Another wink and he turned back to his job.

Suzy headed on, the quick tap of her heels unheard amid the noise. She carefully avoided the conveyor lines of cartons, the stacks of flour and sugar sacks leaning against each other on metal pallets, and the sudden, startling advance of the fork-lifts. A pretty young woman, her ponytail sticking out from beneath her hard hat, zipped by in a little go-cart, its back loaded with boxes labeled Kevin's Kookies. Someday, Suzy wondered, would *her* picture be on that label? On billboards? On nationwide TV screens during the commercial break for *The Cosby Show*? Oh, yes, she thought, grinning. Yes, yes, yes! She could feel it. Today was her lucky day. . . .

Or would be, she added, groaning as she slowed to a halt, if she could only get to this interview!

The entire back wall of the warehouse was covered with doors. Wide ones, narrow ones, all unlabeled!

"This is *not* fair," Suzy muttered aloud. She pushed back her thick hair, which now curled rebelliously against the nape of her neck from an uncontrollable flush of nervousness. The start of a headache fluttered just above her eyes. Clutching her portfolio tightly, she marched over to the nearest workman.

"Excuse me," she said, letting out a sigh of ill-concealed exasperation, "but could you *please* tell me which is Mr. Ross's office?"

The fellow continued to shift flour sacks from one table to another.

Suzy cleared her throat, raised her voice, and just about yelled, "Pardon me, but where is Mr. Ross's office?"

He didn't budge.

She put a hand lightly on his arm. He turned and dusted the front of her dress and her nose with a good helping of flour.

Suzy's eyes shot wide open, then she burst into surprised laughter. And when the workman, already blushing, dazzled, and wide-eyed, started to brush off the front of her, she collapsed into giggles.

"That's all right, really, I'll get it," she said. "If you could just please tell me where Mr. Ross's office is . . ."

He sent flour flying in a dusty arc toward the door at the far left.

"You're sure?" she teased, making his blush deepen.

He nodded, shy and silent, but as she walked away he gave a piercing, if off-key, wolf whistle.

Suzy gulped. Even with the blast of noise at her back, there was no missing that sharp signal of sexual approval. Now her own cheeks were flaming, but there was no turning back. With the flat of one hand she tried to brush away the comet's trail of flour across her breasts. White flour on sapphire silk . . . it was hopeless! She rubbed the tip of her nose, gazed ruefully at the unmarked door in front of her, and gave it three good hard raps.

Was that a "come in" she heard? Who could tell? "Well, here goes everything!" she whispered, and stepped into the office.

"Hello!" she said loudly. "Mr. Ross, I'm Suzy Keller and I'm here for the interview—"

Her voice echoed around the quiet, beautifully paneled office.

"Oh, goodness," she whispered, her blush spreading downward across her throat and breasts. For a moment she closed her eyes, wishing she could start this day over.

The two men in the office stood mesmerized.

One was a handsome blond in a suit and tie standing just behind the desk. The other was taller, darker, broader, compelling even in jeans and a T-shirt as he leaned against the wall.

But it was the blond who broke the silence and drew Suzy's attention. "Ms. Keller? We weren't expecting you until Monday. Your agency called to postpone—"

"Oh, they weren't supposed to! I decided to come out on my own, and now I'm probably interrupting something important, but, Mr. Ross, I was just afraid someone else would show up for the interview today and you'd hire her and I really think I am perfect for this job. I *know* I am! Here." She quickly placed her leather folder on the desk before him and slipped out a breathtaking series of eight by ten glossies. "If you'll just take a look at my portfolio—"

The blond's brows jumped in appreciation, but his voice was steady. "Whoa! Ms. Keller, I would *love* to look at your portfolio! I'd even like to borrow it for a day . . . or a week. But you may rescind the offer when I tell you I am not Mr. Ross. I'm Mike Pepper, and I'm yours if you ever need a lawyer. But this"—he pointed across the room—"this lucky fella is Kevin Ross."

Suzy turned her emerald gaze to the silent man in the corner and, as her eyes met his, her heart took a quick little leap up to her throat and then down to her toes. He was gorgeous. Not pretty like the men she was often paired with in the ads, not even like those at the endless parties and dinners she attended at her agent's insistence. But solid. Dark and solid and strong-looking, with thick black hair over deep dark eyes. Straight, determined brows and the start of worry lines around his eyes and at the sides of his mouth. A beautiful mouth, which even as she stared lifted into a wide, easy grin.

The grin startled her, teased her, and she began talking again, just to cover her surprise. "Mr. Ross, I'm so glad to meet you. And I hope I'm not interrupting anything, but as I said, I really think I would do a terrific job as the Kevin's Kookies girl. I've done many food commercials before— breakfast cereal, hot dogs, even tortillas. Here, would *you* like to see my portfolio?" She took a quick step toward him and thrust the pictures into his hands, aware of the brush of her fingertips against his, feeling suddenly dizzy and giddy and happy.

"And, Mr. Ross," she went on hurriedly, "I know I should let my agent tell you all these good things about me, but since she's not here, I'll just mention that I'm very versatile, and can appeal to the family audience as well as present a more sophisticated image, and even appear quite a number of years younger—or older!—if your marketing campaign should require that. See?" In one quick gesture she pushed her heavy bangs back off her face and caught the fiery sweep of her hair into a knot at the nape of her neck. She smiled up into his dark eyes.

His smile broadened but, unaccountably, hers wobbled just the tiniest bit.

Nerves, she chided herself silently. Calm down! Just be confident, poised. . . . You've done this all before! "I think you would be pleased, Mr. Ross, with both my publicity photos and my tapings . . . as well as any personal appearances the job might require. And . . ." She paused, praying that he would say something, anything, but he seemed to be enjoying himself too darn much, so she rushed on, undaunted. "*And* if you would like to see any particular walk or stance . . . ?" Still talking, she turned and began to circle the room, moving with the languid grace of long practice.

Mike Pepper's laugh cut her short. "Whoa again! Here, sit down. Take it easy." He pulled the chair out from behind the desk. "Now, go on and tell him everything you want, but you've got to face him. Kevin's deaf."

"What?" Her eyes widened in surprise as they shot from Mike to Kevin, then back again. Her voice softened in awe. "I can't believe it. He's done *all* this and he's deaf?" Admiration shone like a clear light that she turned on Kevin's face.

Caught by her gaze, it was Kevin's turn to blush and he did, a dark, handsome flush that Suzy knew didn't stop at the top of his T-shirt. Oh, he had beautiful shoulders. And a strong, broad chest. Tilting her head to the side, she smiled at him. "Sorry. I didn't mean to embarrass you. It's just . . . Well, I think you must be quite amazing. This is a big business you've built here, single-handedly . . . or so my agent said. And—" Her hand flew to her mouth in sudden comprehension. "And all your employees are deaf also! That explains the flying carton . . . and my run-in with the flour sack!" She touched her fingertips absentmindedly to the front of her dress, her concentration locked on the man in front of her. "Amazing." Then she realized she was staring and felt the blood rise to her cheeks. She straightened her skirt and settled her hands demurely in her lap. "I mean, Mr. Ross, you're much different than I expected for a man of your accomplishments."

His laugh was low and husky and exciting.

Suzy's face relaxed into a charming smile. "I want you to know I practiced that line . . . or at least something like it! You . . . you're reading my lips, aren't you? Oh, my. Do I look all right?"

"Fantastic!" he signed, throwing both hands up, palms pulsing out twice, as if in wonder.

"I understood that!" she said excitedly, leaning forward in her chair. "That means wonderful, great . . . right?"

He nodded, smiling, his gaze playing lightly across her face.

"See? I *told* you I was perfect for this job. A girlfriend of mine in high school was deaf, and she taught me sign language. Look: *I know how to sign*," she said in slow, rusty signs. "Not 'fantastic.' " She laughed, mimicking his earlier sign. "But a little . . . a start! Right?"

Grinning, Kevin nodded. What else could he do? She was so damned positive, and optimistic . . . and charming. She was irresistible.

The thought caused him a low stirring of discomfort. For just a second longer he let himself wonder what it would be like . . . Like magic? Like a dream? Then his grin faded and he crossed his arms firmly over his chest. Watch out, Ross, he told himself. Don't play with fire if you don't want to get burned!

"Mike," he signed in sharp, blunt gestures. "Tell her what I say. Tell her thank you for coming, and we'll be sure to let her know. But tell her I—I had another look in mind. Something more ordinary. Ponytail and a T-shirt. Girl-next-door kind of thing— "

"But I *was* the girl next door!" Suzy interrupted, her temper rising with her disappointment. "Right next door to Harry Wilson. Right on Elm Street. Backyard swings and barbecues. Baseball games on the vacant lot on the corner. Lemonade stands. I can do it! Really. I'll be any look you want me to be."

Kevin felt his resolve weaken. She was so spirited, so full of pluck and determination and honesty. Those were feelings *he* sure as hell could identify with, and yet—

But before he could say or do anything, a light flashed over the door. Saved by the bell! he thought.

The welcome interruption was the kind of problem he had *no* trouble dealing with: a jammed conveyor belt and an angry foreman. Mike followed Kevin out the door with a quick "Excuse us. Emergency—" and Suzy was left alone in the office.

She wasn't going to get the job. She knew it. She could always tell, just as she could always tell which pose a client would select, or which photographer would give her a bad time. Model's instinct. She was loaded with instinct for this business, born with it as surely as with her blaze of red hair and wide green eyes. That's what had made it all so easy, why it was *her* they picked and not the other two-year-olds, and ten-year-olds, and twelve-year-olds when her mother dragged her from agency to agency, from job to job. It was why her mother *did* the dragging, so sure Suzy would be a star. Another Suzy Parker, her mother believed with the unshakable faith of Moses.

But Suzy was *not* going to get this job.

"And I *want* this job," she grumbled softly, setting her hands on her hips. She nibbled unhappily on her lower lip as she thought of the nationwide magazine campaign, the prime-time TV spots, the thousands, no . . . maybe *hundreds of thousands* of cookie boxes on hundreds of thousands of grocery store shelves.

Not to mention that man. If she didn't get the job, she'd never see him again.

"Hmmm . . ." She narrowed her eyes, thinking, warming to the problem. For a moment she had had him. For a moment she had perfectly matched the fantasy in his head. Or better, she had awoken a fantasy he hadn't even admitted to himself. She had seen it in those smoke-dark eyes: a gleam, a spark! She had seen the muscles jump along the hard lines of his jaw. Then good old reason, or caution, or guardedness had intervened.

And there went her chance at being the Kevin's Kookies girl.

Well, the show wasn't over until the curtain fell, she decided with a sudden flash of determination. Pacing the thickly carpeted floor, she did a quick run-through of the contents of the office. And there on a shelf was just what she was looking for. T-shirts. White, black, red, yellow, blue . . . all emblazoned with Kevin's logo. Without a moment's hesitation she slipped out of her dress, folded it across the back of his chair, then placed her slip on top of it. The air-conditioning made goose bumps rise along her arms and down the long, silky curve of her back. Her nipples puckered. Quickly she tugged a T-shirt off its pile, one as red as an apple for the teacher or a teenager's blush. If Kevin Ross wanted the girl next door, that's just what she'd give him! A ponytail? Fine! Dropping the T-shirt for the moment, she rummaged in her purse and found her hairbrush. A few vigorous strokes and her hair was waving happily in her hand, as perky a tail as anyone could wish for, the few loose ends curling at her neck with independent energy. Now, she thought, a rubber band . . . ? There was one, holding snug a roll of papers on his desk. She set a paperweight on top of the curling sheets, snapped the rubber band into place, and fluffed her bangs. Then she picked up the T-shirt again and began to put it on. She was just pulling the lower edge down over her breasts when the door opened and Kevin stepped inside.

He saw the ripe curve of her breast, the golden plane of her abdomen, her baby blue bikini bottoms strung across perfect hips, and the lovely length of her legs. "Oh, Lord . . ." he breathed, and this time she read *his* lips.

Kevin slammed the door shut and leaned back against it, his broad chest rising and falling, his hands clenched.

Suzy didn't know if he was guarding the door in boyish shock or out of some gallant notion of chivalry. But it didn't matter. It tickled her, she who was so completely comfortable in her body, so used to its lines and shape and texture that she took it completely for granted. And the people she worked with also took it for granted, interested in her beauty only as far as it suited their shampoo, their clothes, their luggage.

"It's all right," she said easily, smoothing the hem of the cotton T-shirt down across the tops of her thighs. "Please don't be embarrassed—"

"Embarrassed?" he signed, not caring if she understood or not. He strode forward, still signing. "This is my office, not a dressing room. I'm not embarrassed. I'm furious!"

That she understood!

"But, Mr. Ross, I—"

"What?" he challenged her with infuriating coolness.

Suzy stepped right up to him, toe to toe, so close that her breasts almost touched his chest. Her bangs brushed his chin as she looked up at him.

"Mr. Ross, I want this job. I'd be the perfect Kevin's Kookies girl and I know it. And you know it! And you're not going to scare me away, and now you know that too! I apologize for changing in your office, but if I had asked, *if* I had explained, you would have told Mr. Pepper to tell me to get lost—"

"Now, wait—"

"Oh, not like that, of course." She waved away his objection, ignoring the gathering thunder of his frown. "You would have been quite polite, but it would have ended up the same way. And it would be a mistake. *Your* mistake. So really . . ." She spaced her words out, letting her mischievous smile shine through. "I'm only looking out for your best interests."

Humor flickered in the depths of his dark eyes. "Thank you very much," he signed, taking a step back to open some space between them. But it was just a small step, a small space, close enough for him to smell the sweetness of her breath, her subtle perfume. "So, you think you're the one for this job?"

Her gaze flew from his hands to her face. "Yes!"

"*I* think you're going to be a lot of trouble, Ms. Keller."

"But I am worth it, Mr. Ross!"

He lifted one dark brow in mock disbelief, but a small still voice in his heart told him she was right. The question was, was *he* prepared to pay the price?

For less than a second he glanced around his

familiar office, but it was changed already. From now until forever he would see the image of her tugging his T-shirt down over her lithe, golden body, her clothes tossed over his chair. He didn't know if he was lucky . . . or damned.

"All right," he said in surrender. "The job is yours. You will be my Kevin's Kookies girl."

"Wonderful decision!" Suzy grinned, wishing she had a cap to fling in the air. Instead, she hugged herself tightly, feeling happiness bubble like champagne in her veins. "Oh, we'll be *great* together, wait and see!" She did a little dancing step toward her clothes, then turned back to Kevin. "I have just one more question: Why didn't you ask for a model who could sign?"

Kevin laughed. "And just how many do you think there are?"

"Just one!" She smiled. "And you've got her! Kismet!"

Two

For the first time in over a year Suzy Keller was up and dressed and out of her apartment before noon on a Saturday morning by choice rather than necessity. It felt terrific. There was no schedule to keep, no director to please, no pose to assume. She could just slip into her skinny black jeans and an oversize cotton shirt à la Audrey Hepburn, wearing no more makeup than mascara and a touch of lipstick. Instead of blush, there were two spots of pure excitement high on her cheeks.

All morning she had tried to curb that excitement, but like a new puppy it leaped and bounded around in her chest, jumping back out at her when she least expected it. She couldn't drink her coffee. She barely felt her shower, even when she turned the water to cold. Thirty minutes of working out with Jane didn't help at all.

It was the job, she told herself. She was going to be the Kevin's Kookies girl, with her face on billboards and in magazine ads and on TV. "That's you!" people would say, and she'd smile graciously and sign their box of chocolate chunk cookies, or

16

their lemon crunch, or their fudge brownie su-
premes. The thought had made her laugh, and
she was still giggling when her mother had called.

"It's the job!" Suzy had told her. "I can't believe
how lucky I am."

"You make your own luck, darling," her mother
had answered, her voice filled with love and pride.

"It's my new job!" Suzy had explained when the
doorman noticed the sparkle in her emerald eyes.

But it was even more than that. It was something else too.

That unnamed something made her knees feel
like water when she stepped from the cab in front
of Kevin's factory just before ten. For a moment
she had to lean back against the dented, dusty
door, waiting for her pulse to slow, unaware that
the poor cabbie's was racing at a gallop.

"You okay, miss?" he asked. "Can I get you
something? A cuppa coffee? A mink coat?"

"Pardon?" Suzy asked, blinking in confusion.
Then she blessed him with one of her heart-stopping smiles. "Oh, no, I'm fine, thank you. But it
was nice of you to offer. 'Bye . . ." With a little
wave she headed for the front door.

She let it slam shut behind her, knowing one
more sound among all the din and clamor wouldn't
make a bit of difference. What a racket! Would she
ever get used to so much noice, ever stop feeling it
reverberate in the marrow of her bones? How amazing to think that all these people, all these attractive, energetic people—the foreman, the packers,
the bakers, the ponytailed girl driving the fork-
lift across the warehouse floor—were all deaf. Their
lives were so different from hers. Things she took
for granted they'd never know: the sound of a
friend's voice, the soft tap of rain on a porch roof,
the clear beauty of Mozart. But perhaps they knew

things she didn't. Perhaps they perceived the world more keenly through other senses. . . .

Like a child involved in a new game, Suzy lost herself in concentration. She pushed away the rumble of noise that filled the warehouse until it was nothing more than background static, then let her gaze drift slowly around, waiting to see what would happen. First she noticed the smells. Warm, sweet smells of baking drifted out from the kitchens: cookie dough and icing, chocolate . . . and lemon . . . and some wonderfully pungent aroma. What? She breathed deeply, closing her eyes to think better. What? Cinnamon? Yes! Rich and spicy!

Pleased, she grinned and looked around the room, noticing for the first time the posters on the walls, colorful blowups of cookies on platters, cookies with milk, cookie jars shaped like teddy bears and mice, cookies melted on children's fingers or packed into lunchboxes, even cookies by candlelight. And the support columns and doorframes were painted in bold, primary colors, rainbow colors. And the people . . . Why, everyone was *talking*! She realized it now, seeing it because she had let herself really look. In the midst of all the lifting, carrying, packing, shelving, everyone was talking, their hands carrying on a constant flowing conversation in sign. An older man challenged another to a game of checkers over lunch. A young woman told a friend about her baby's new tooth. A young man flirted with the ponytailed girl, asking her to go bowling on Sunday night.

Suzy hid her smile and drew her gaze away, not wanting to eavesdrop. How amazing this was, exciting and wonderful. And Kevin Ross had made it all happen.

The thought struck her like a bolt of lightning, and she felt weak-kneed again, her head spinning. Kevin Ross. Because of him, each of these people had a job. No, *more* than a job: a future and pride and dignity. She had been working long enough to know that it wasn't easy, not for anyone, but certainly it couldn't be for these deaf men and women. And here was this business, this incredibly successful business, built by this incredible man.

A little shiver of excitement walked up and down her spine, the same unexpected excitement that had awakened her much too early this morning.

"Kevin Ross . . ." she whispered aloud, smiling. "You may be just the most intriguing hunk of man I've ever met."

And with a toss of her blazing hair, she headed for Kevin's office.

He wasn't there.

She stood at the back of the factory, wondering where to look next. She knew he had to be around somewhere. Mike Pepper had warned her that not only did the boss work most Saturdays, but the whole crew was gung-ho. Weekends, evenings, holidays—anything for Kevin. "He's a regular slave driver," Mike had teased, landing a light punch on his pal's shoulder. "Not to mention a ferocious racquetball player, a daredevil sailor, a wicked bass fisherman . . . and he cheats at Monopoly!"

Suzy laughed again at the memory.

But now, where to find him? Pushing her hair back behind one ear, she headed for the kitchen. She peeked in, catching the startled but appreciative eye of the nearest baker.

"Hi!" she said, and signed. "I'm looking for Mr. Ross. Is he here today?"

The man watched her, his gaze wandering from her slow-moving hands to her perfect figure. With a broad grin he pointed back across the warehouse to a pair of double doors that opened and closed continually, each time revealing a slice of blue sky beyond.

"Oh, the loading dock? Thanks."

Suzy wove her way through the room, a tall, stunning red-haired woman whose walk sizzled with enough sensuality to heat the entire warehouse.

When she stepped out through the swinging doors, the sunlight caught fire in her hair and turned her skin to gold. The workmen on the dock nearly fell right off to the pavement below. The truck drivers turned, one at a time like a row of dominoes, to stare openmouthed. But Suzy was oblivious to all the gaping and admiration.

"Ooooh, this heat!" she murmured, fanning the humid air away from her face with one hand, her gaze searching for Kevin. A chorus of ready agreement rose from the others and she looked around, startled to find herself the center of so much attention. Quickly she smiled and headed farther on down the platform, still looking for Kevin.

She stopped to watch the trucks pulls in, raise their folding doors, and swallow up the cartons and cartons of cookies. KEVIN's KOOKIES. And *she* was a part of that now. She tossed her head back and smiled at the cloudless sky until her vision was blocked by a huge semi that backed up to the loading dock. Doors banged, boots shuffled across wooden planks, and Suzy stepped into the welcoming coolness of the building's shadow to watch as the boxes were piled into the truck.

As if lured by her thoughts, Kevin rounded the front end of the truck just then, faded jeans riding low on his lean hips. Suzy straightened up. My, he was nice to look at! she thought. Beads of perspiration glistened across his tanned brow as he hoisted several boxes up onto the lip of a truck, his muscles bulging like a weight-lifter's beneath the strain. His T-shirt worked its way free of his jeans, giving her a glimpse of the bronzed body beneath. His thick dark hair ruffled across his forehead as a breeze found its way to the back of the old brick warehouse.

Suzy didn't make a move to announce her presence. She just stood in the shadows and watched him with a keen and rising enjoyment.

Her vision was blocked for a moment by a harassed, stocky man who hurried over to Kevin, his hands flying through the air.

Kevin reached out and silenced him, capturing the man's arms between his hands. "It's okay, Gus," he signed, a lopsided smile creasing his face. "I know we're two hours late, but the new batch of boxes will be out in a minute. Don't worry. I'll stick around this afternoon and help."

The man breathed a sigh of relief and wiped the sweat from his brow. "Thanks, boss," he signed gratefully, and hurried back to his work.

Kevin shoved his hands into his jeans pockets, and stood watching all the activity for a moment, his feet apart, a pleased smile playing across his mouth. Life was good, he thought. Business was better than he'd ever imagined. Why, even on a Saturday, Mike had just told him, they'd gotten inquiries on more franchises. It seemed that every shopping center this side of New York wanted Kevin's Kookies! Kevin shook his head and laughed. Who'd have ever thought a street kid would have become a cookie king?

Suzy watched the smile spread from his eyes across his handsome face and wondered what he was thinking. Was he thinking of her? Maybe . . . No, she shouldn't expect that—yet! But she'd soon weave herself into Kevin Ross's thoughts, oh, yes, she would!

Her gaze followed his movements as he dropped

from the dock in one athletic leap. Seconds later, a dozen boxes rumbled down the ramp. As if they were filled with cotton balls, he scooped up two at a time and shoved them into the back of the truck, then slammed the heavy door shut and slipped the chain lock into place. With a grin and an "okay" sign, he waved to the driver, turned, and swung himself back up on the ramp.

The heavy gears were a grinding disturbance to no one but Suzy, and she watched as the driver pulled out several feet, then shifted to reverse in order to make the turn down the alley. One of the young men Suzy had noticed earlier jumped off the ramp to collect the empty boxes and packing scraps that were left scattered in the truck's wake. His slim back was bent over, and Suzy smiled at his dedication, then looked up to see where Kevin had gone. But she saw only the huge truck slowly backing into the area where the boy knelt, invisible to the driver.

"Watch out!" she screamed as she stood frozen on the other side of the ramp. "Move!" The boy didn't lift his head an inch, just continued to pick up the litter. Oh, Lord, he couldn't hear her! Suzy's stomach lurched, and her heart leaped to her throat in terror as she began to run along the ramp, knowing there was no way she could reach the boy or the driver in time. "Stop! Stop! Oh, no—"

Kevin seemed to fly out of nowhere, his lean, muscular body uncoiling in midair like a panther's as he threw himself off the dock and into the truck's path. He caught the boy by his shoulders, shoving him over to the side before the kid ever had a chance to stand up. Kevin rolled after him out of danger's way.

Suzy didn't move or breathe, just stood there

with her hands covering her open mouth, her eyes stinging with held-back tears.

Kevin and the boy lay in a jumbled heap on the pavement as the truck driver lazily screeched his gears into forward and moved along, never noticing the chaos he left behind. Suzy walked unsteadily to the edge of the dock, slipped down over the side, and stood pressed against the sun-baked concrete.

"Are you hurt?" she asked, her hands signing clumsily, her eyes wide with fear. "Are you both okay?"

Kevin looked up at her. Where had she come from? he wondered. What made the light shine that way through her hair? A fan of laugh lines appeared at the corners of his eyes as he smiled. "The question is," he teased, "am I in heaven? Are you an angel?" He sketched wings in the bright air, and his dark tousled hair fell over his forehead, making him look like a boy rather than a twenty-eight-year-old businessman.

"No, just a nervous employee who thought she had seen the last of her new boss!" Suzy grinned and knelt to check the teenager's bruises. He blushed beneath her ministrations and tried to step aside, but Suzy was adamant. "Your elbows . . ." She looked at him intently and touched the red scrapes that sliced raggedly across his skin. "We should clean these." Her brows lifted up into a sweep of coppery hair. "And you—" She looked at Kevin. "You are wonderful! Superman!" And though she stumbled over the signs, her eyes held a message Kevin couldn't fail to see.

It made his blood race like fire through his veins. It made his whole body tighten with desire. It *almost* made him forget reality—which was a very dangerous thing to let happen, Kevin knew. With forced casualness he stood up, shrugged, and brushed the gravel off his jeans. "What are you doing here on a Saturday morning?"

Suzy laughed lightly and matched his shrug. "Thought I'd just come in and get a feel for the product," she answered. "I take my work very seriously."

A grin twitched at the corner of Kevin's mouth. He signed something to the boy, who immediately went off to the first aid room, then motioned for Suzy to follow him as he wove his way around the boxes and into the bustling factory. He led her to a tiny, cluttered office close to his own. A robust older woman with twinkling eyes sat at the desk, surrounding by phones and filing cabinets. Kevin paused for introductions.

"Ethel, this is my Kookie girl," he signed, grinning. "Suzy Keller, Ethel Standish, my secretary." When he signed their names, he finger-spelled them first, slowly, for clarity, then gave each a name sign. Ethel's sign was an *E* written into his left palm. For Suzy he paused a moment, narrowing his eyes, his gaze unreadable, then signed an *S* over his heart.

"So you're the one!" Ethel said, her smile open and friendly. "Well, Suzy, we're thrilled to have you aboard. And I can sure see why the boss hired you. I bet you'll sell a million cookies! And Mike Pepper says you sign . . . ?"

Suzy nodded happily. "I'm not great at it, but I learn quickly."

"Terrific!" Ethel shuffled some papers and her glance drew Suzy's around the cluttered office. "Well, I'd better be getting back to work, or the boss will keep me chained to my desk for the entire weekend! Real slave driver," she teased, throwing Kevin an affectionate smile.

"Christmas rush!" Kevin's sign countered. He

took Suzy's elbow and directed her into his office, then closed the door behind them.

A fleeting image of her half-in, half-out of a red T-shirt popped into his mind, but he pushed it quickly away. "Iced tea?" he asked, gesturing toward a round table near the window.

Suzy nodded and settled herself into one of the two chairs while Kevin dropped ice from a small refrigerator into two tall glasses. He filled the glasses with tea and added a lemon slice to each.

"So," Suzy said as he sat down across from her, "here we are." She leaned her elbows on the table and cupped her chin in her palms, her sparkling eyes absorbing the strong, rugged lines of his face. "I want to know *everything* I need to know about your company. I want to do a terrific job for you, Kevin." The words spilled from her beautiful lips, and Kevin understood what she was saying. His only trouble was keeping his mind on work.

As he began to tell her what she wanted to know, he moved his hands slowly so she could follow, finger-spelling when a sign was too difficult for her. He was intense and patient, his eyes lit with a contagious enthusiasm. "It's easy," he signed. "We've got the next couple of years mapped out: marketing plans, a timetable for growth and development. Franchises across the country. Let me show you where you fit in."

He leaned back and pulled several sheets of paper from his desk, then spread them on the table between them. It was his public relations firm's plan for Kevin's Kookies, the carefully worked out strategy that would make his cookies a household word within the year. And Suzy fit there, he told her, pointing to the papers, right at the heart of everything. "You'll be my 'front man,' " he signed, and winked, "the one who sells the success story, the one who charms the public. We're going to launch—" He paused and changed the sign to "start," but soon got caught up in the excitement again. "We're going to start an extensive ad campaign. Lots of media coverage. And as new markets open, and the franchising operation grows, there will be even more public appearances."

He looked up into her wide, serious green eyes and knew without a doubt that no one could do it better. "You'll be my voice," he said. "My chief representative."

Suzy watched the broad movements of his hands as they swept through the air. The meaning of the gestures flowed from them like magic.

"Fantastic," she said, leaning back and crossing her long, jean-clad legs. "That's just what I was hoping for. We'll make each other famous! And I promise . . ." She carefully touched her index finger to her lips, then placed her right palm against her closed left hand. "I promise, Kevin, you won't be sorry you hired me."

She chatted on at a snail's pace, seasoning her words with her own improvised signs along the way so that Kevin started to laugh and missed some of what she was saying, but it didn't matter to him at all. She was lovely, free, and funny. Her being here changed the whole pattern of his day. No other Saturday had ever felt like this. Finally she paused and sat back, her face flushed, and wrapped her fingers around the chilled tea glass. "Your turn," she said with a grin, and drank her tea slowly, watching Kevin the whole time.

"Let me just say that I think you'll be a wonderful addition to our crew."

She set the glass down and leaned forward, eager to understand each movement. "That last word . . ." She repeated the sign, moving her hands in a circle as he had done. "I didn't quite get it. Help me. I want to learn everything."

"C-r-e-w," he finger-spelled for her, then drew his C-shaped hands in a circle again.

She nodded. "Okay, got it! Now, Kevin, tell me about you. How did you end up here in this factory, making cookies and becoming famous?"

Her eagerness spilled from her eyes like sunlight, and Kevin grinned at her floundering efforts. The sign for "factory" had given way to that of "department store."

"What is so funny?" Suzy signed more carefully. One perfect brow arched above her emerald eyes as she glared at him.

"Nothing," he signed back, biting off the tail end of his grin.

"No, go ahead and tell me," she insisted. "Did I make the wrong sign?"

He let his gaze linger on her face for just one second more, feeling his heart hammer against his ribs. Then he shifted his glance to her lovely hands and shook his head. "You're doing fine, Suzy. Your signs are fine," he answered, taking his open hand and touching his thumb to his broad chest.

Suzy's gaze followed his movement and settled there on that chest, a little smile curving her lips. His T-shirt was stretched tight across his hard, well-defined muscles and a mass of dark hair curled over the ribbed neck. There was absolutely no disguising the fact that he had a very good body! She finally tore her gaze away and looked back into his sparkling eyes, lifting one shoulder in a little shrug. "So, what is so funny, boss?"

"I was just thinking that at the speed we're talking, we'll have to stop for lunch between sentences. One conversation could last until midnight."

She laughed, a sweet high sound that he couldn't hear, but almost felt. "Sorry. I'm a little rusty, I guess. And I thought it would be easier for you if I went slowly. I know I really have to—" She paused, frowning, but couldn't remember how to say *concentrate* and quickly substituted words. ". . . watch carefully to catch all of your signs."

"Practice makes perfect. What word were you looking for?"

She finger-spelled c-o-n-c-e-n-t-r-a-t-e and he demonstrated the sign, reaching across the table and taking her slim hand in his own and guiding her through the gesture. Her hand was as cool as silk, but he felt a surprising heat race up his arm. He drew his hand away, but Suzy quickly signed "Show me again," and slipped her hand back into his. Mischief danced behind her eyes.

A wry grin tugged at the corner of his mouth. He showed her the sign again, their eyes locked, then he released her hand and set his firmly on the table.

"Thanks," she said, her mind toying with the surprising pleasure of his touch. It was probably time for her to go. She was keeping him from his work. Loading cookies, helping the men. Paperwork, maybe. Her mind hopped from one thing to another. And *she* had things to do too. Gobs! The weekly cleaning of her tiny apartment, a mile-long string of Saturday errands before dinner with the folks that night, her agent's phone calls to answer. But all she wanted to do in the wide world was sit exactly where she was, talking with Kevin Ross.

A smile tipped her lips. "So, besides being slow, what other faults do I have?"

"None that I can see," he answered gallantly, knowing he was getting in too deep, but unable to resist her. Then he shook his head, raked his fingers through his dark hair, and folded his arms stubbornly across his chest.

Suzy dropped her chin into her hands and smiled at him, and in a moment he found himself signing again, even before he knew he was going to. "You need to be more relaxed when you sign. Most of the signs are correct, but they're stiff. You're not letting them show what you're thinking or feeling. Signing is like any other language, full of emotion and meaning that goes beyond the words themselves. Watch."

He thought for a moment, hesitating, then signed, "You are very pretty," his hand circling his face.

Before she could do more than blush, he waved the air clear and continued with a glint in his dark eyes. "You are beautiful!" he signed, another quick circle ending with a flourish as though he had gathered stardust in his hand and flung it up against a velvet sky.

He could feel the sweat under his arms, across his chest, but he was going to brazen this out now, and the consequences be damned.

"In sign," he continued, staring into the depths of her wide green eyes, "you can shout, whisper, plead, demand, cry . . ." His hands cut through the space between them, trembling, swooping, chopping out the words as the emotions swept across his handsome face.

Suzy found herself trembling, awed by the power of the man.

"And that's not all!" he exclaimed, etching the mark on the air itself. "You can watch my face, my body. Sign is like theater. It uses all you have to give, all you are willing to bare." He stopped and drew a harsh breath between clenched teeth. Cool it, Ross, he told himself, before you make a complete fool of yourself! Damn, he cursed silently. He hadn't meant to say so much. What did he think he was trying to prove?

Suzy sat wide-eyed, silent, for just another second, then she carefully pushed back her chair, stood up, leaned across the table, and kissed him right on the mouth.

Kevin tasted the satin of her lips, the warm, sweet pressure against his mouth that made his body tighten from his toes up. He opened one eye and saw the dark fringe of her lashes brushing the perfect curve of her cheek. Shutting his eyes tight to lock that beautiful image in his head, he kissed her back, brushing his lips softly against hers.

When they both dropped back into their chairs, Kevin signed with a whisper, "You *are* a surprise."

And Suzy understood exactly what he meant.

Three

She'd be wearing something soft and clinging, black, maybe—no, pale gold, the color of fine champagne—and she'd leave her shoulders bare. Perhaps even her back, the dress dipping down beneath the fine wings of her shoulder blades, her skin all golden, satin to the touch. And her hair would be like a flame he'd dare to take in his hands. They'd dance. Yes. And she'd be all slim and golden in his arms, and his fingers would lie cool on the hollow of her back. Her hair would brush his cheek. Yes . . . He'd hold her gently, but close, so close against him that he'd feel the rapid beating of her heart, and her breasts would press against his chest. He'd hold her and they'd turn and sway and the music would be soft and low . . .

Hell! It was *his* daydream. If he wanted music, he could have music! Right?

Right, Ross! He nodded solemnly at his reflection in the mirror. Then an ironic grin curved the corners of his mouth. Letting his gaze travel down the mirror, he shook his head. If you want them even to let you in the door, he told himself, you'd better take a cold shower, Romeo!

Later, when he was straightening his bow tie above the starched white pleats of his tuxedo shirt, he met his own dark gaze again. Wouldn't it be nice, he thought, not to be alone? To have someone to straighten his tie . . . smile at over coffee . . . share his bed.

Well, a man could dream. No one could be hurt by a dream. . . .

Here he was on his way to this party, the kind of posh, black-tie affair no one would even let him park cars for as a kid. Amazing! And this was *his* party. His, to celebrate all those years of sweat and determination, all the good friends who had stood by him, the sweet taste of success. And to introduce to the world his Kevin's Kookies girl.

There. It all came back to that again. Suzy was what had him dreaming. All the money and success and celebration in the world wouldn't satisfy him now. But a dance, with her in his arms . . . Even though it could only be one dance, a dance to dream on.

Across town, Suzy shivered unexpectedly. She rubbed the goose bumps off her bare arms, leaned her chin on her hands, and drifted into the delicious world of her own fantasy.

He'd turn, scan the room with his bold, commanding gaze, and see her. His dark, smoldering eyes, full of magic, would light with a secret pleasure. He'd smile. She'd smile back, her heart thudding at the sight of him, his dark sensuality tamed for the moment by the elegance of his tuxedo. But his glance would be fierce and wild. Nodding to the others, he'd stride across the room and take her in his arms. Yes, she'd whisper. Yes. She'd feel the crush of his starched shirt against her breast. His broad shoulders would need no padding in the tuxedo jacket, and she'd slip her hand up his back, feeling the heat of him through his shirt. She would hear the wild pounding of his heart above the music of the orchestra as they danced . . .

Heck! It was her daydream, wasn't it? If she wanted smoldering eyes and a wildly pounding heart, she could have it! Right?

Right, Suzy Keller! She grinned at her reflection. You bet your boots you can! The only question was, could she make it happen? Was there some fairy dust to borrow? A first star to wish on? A rabbit's foot to rub? Or, my dear lovestruck girl, she asked herself, do you just trust to fate?

Well, the least she could do was give fate a helping hand. Reaching for a little crystal bottle, she dabbed Joy behind her ears and knees, and a little more in the pale valley between her breasts.

But her hands were shaking. Why did this seem so important, as if her whole life depended on it? She knew it was silly, but it was exactly how she felt: trembling, hopeful, suddenly shy. Leaning her forehead against the cool glass of her mirror, she breathed a silent prayer.

Then she turned to where her dress lay waiting on her bed. She unwrapped the tissue that swathed it and pulled out a pale-gold chiffon gown, the color of fine champagne, that bared one shoulder and made her feel absolutely beautiful. The long skirt rustled and whispered, promising magic and romance. Suzy smiled. Maybe she'd get her wishes yet. . . .

Suzy sat in the back of the limousine and watched the chauffeur climb the steps to Lorraine Barr's front door. A knock, a pause, and her agent appeared, dressed to perfection as always and wearing her "the world is my oyster" look that Suzy adored but could never quite imitate.

"Hello, Suzy," Lorraine said as she stepped into the backseat. "Oh, you do look lovely. A perfect choice. We do want heads to turn tonight, don't we?" She settled into the plush seat and laid a hand confidentially on Suzy's arm. "I am just dying to meet this Mr. Ross. You've certainly got my curiosity piqued, all this secrecy and blushes. There!" She gave a brassy laugh. "You're doing it again."

Suzy pressed a hand to her cheek and, yes, she was hot enough to melt wax. "It's just all the excitement," she said quickly. "The party, the campaign. And did I tell you that all the local TV stations called? Oh, of course I did, and that lovely gal at the radio station in Fairway—"

"Is this Suzy Keller talking? Veteran of how many campaigns? The girl who's taken Kansas City by storm? Something's different this time, you can't fool me. But if having a secret makes you glow like this, I'm just happy for you, dear."

"Thanks, Lorraine. Oh, we're there!" Suzy caught her lower lip between her teeth and looked up at the shining rooftop of the Alameda Plaza. Her heart did a little somersault into her throat. "Do I look all right? Do I need to fix my lipstick?"

"All you need to do is smile and be yourself. You're irresistible, you know, which is why I love having you for a client. Now, have fun! And relax!"

She could just as easily have sprouted wings!

As soon as the doorman opened the limousine door, a bevy of local reporters and photographers swarmed forward.

"Ms. Keller, over here, please—"

"Ms. Keller, Kevin's Kookies is quite a Kansas

City phenomenon. Was Mr. Ross looking specifically for a hometown girl to represent his product?"

"Ms. Keller, rumor says you were the only model Mr. Ross even considered. Would you like to comment on that?"

"Lucky me!" Suzy said, her emerald eyes sparkling as the light bulbs popped. "But then, they *do* say Mr. Ross is a genius!" And with a toss of her head, she let her flame-bright hair add the exclamation point to tomorrow's headline.

Lorraine gave her an approving nod and then, before another camera could click, Mike Pepper dashed to the rescue. "Suzy, Ms. Barr, the party's waiting for you upstairs." He ushered them into the glass elevator, and they rose along the outside of the hotel, the lights and fountains of the Plaza dwindling below them. Suzy made the introductions, then leaned back against the glass, hoping to catch her breath. For a moment it felt as if she were floating in air, the dark sky all around her, her own excitement carrying her aloft. Mike caught her eye and smiled. "You look absolutely beautiful tonight. Happy?"

"Yes." She laughed, reaching over to hug his arm. "And proud. And nervous."

"You sound just like Kevin! I swear, I've never seen him like this. You two are a pair!"

"Yes, I think so too," she whispered, and ignored his startled look of surprise.

The glass doors swung open, the orchestra stopped playing, and a hush fell over the room.

Kevin heard nothing, but knew immediately that it was Suzy. He turned and saw her. The room blurred. His heart stopped beating. It was as if time itself stopped. But it was inside his head, inside his heart. To everyone else—friends, business associates, the media—he seemed merely to smile and stride quickly across the room to the lovely young woman holding out her hand to him.

He took her hand, slipped it through his arm, and escorted her back across the crowded room. "Ready?" he signed with his free hand.

Suzy nodded, smiling, her gaze lingering on his face. She tried to look elsewhere, at the flower-decked podium waiting ahead, the orchestra, the gathered crowd. Were her parents here yet? Where was Kevin's family? They must be so proud at this moment! She knew *her* mother was flying, held to earth only by her father's more quiet pride.

Talk about pride! she thought, marveling at what she saw next. Each and every one of Kevin's employees, from stock clerk to foreman, was there, gathered in a tight knot at one side of the room. Every face was turned to the boss, and every face shone with pride and confidence and happiness. Ethel dabbed at her eyes with a handkerchief. Gus waved and flashed Suzy a V-for-victory sign.

She answered with a wink and a bold thumbs-up, and a bulb popped, capturing her enthusiasm for posterity. Everyone laughed, including Kevin, and he slipped his arm around her waist and hugged her tight in pleasure. She looked up and met his glance, and the rest of the room disappeared.

When they reached the podium, a wild burst of applause broke from the people standing right up front. "Way t'go, Kevin!" a dark-haired woman, much too young to be his mother, cheered, lifting her hands in the old prizefighter's winning sign. This time Kevin smiled and signed back, then clasped his hands over his head. Through her own suddenly misty eyes Suzy thought she saw an unexpected brightness in his. There was a whole explosion of flashbulbs, bright as fireworks, and when her vision cleared, Kevin was back in perfect control, cool and handsome and totally composed.

Mike joined them at the podium and reached for the microphone. "Ladies and gentlemen, friends, Kevin Ross would like me to thank you all for coming tonight to help him celebrate the success of Kevin's Kookies and to meet his Kevin Kookies girl, Suzy Keller."

Again applause filled the room, echoing off the linen tablecloths and crystal stemware, the red roses and flickering candles. Suzy stepped up to the microphone and began to speak, her eyes shining, her smile dazzling. Kevin had stepped to the side so that he could see her face, and his dark gaze never wavered as she shared a brief history of the company, outlined the campaign they were about to launch, and began to describe his goals for the future. There, on her lips, were his dreams, voiced for all to hear.

So intent was he that he was caught off guard when she turned and smiled directly at him. "And this," she said in a voice that trembled ever so slightly, "is the man who has made this dream a reality. Kevin Ross."

She began to applaud him, her lovely face quite serious now, tears balancing on the thick fringe of her lashes. She stepped back, leaving the podium for Kevin alone.

The crowd loved it. Everyone exploded into applause as Kevin stepped up to the microphone. She could see the color rise over the gleaming-white starched collar of his shirt and spread across his cheeks. Bending his dark head, he answered the crowd with a small, very formal bow. Then he touched the tips of his right hand to his lips and held his hand out to his audience. "Thank you," he said in sign. "Thank you all very much."

The orchestra began to play. People gathered

around to congratulate Kevin, to meet Suzy, to have their pictures taken with one or both.

Out of the corner of her eye, Suzy watched for her parents' entrance. Anxiety warred with the excitement in her heart, leaving her feeling as though all her nerves had been rubbed with sandpaper. Oh, she wanted them to like each other. Please, she prayed silently, let this go well.

"Parties like this are wonderful," someone at her side said, "but they make me feel like I've swallowed a can of worms! How about you?"

Suzy turned and saw it was the dark-haired woman whose "way t'go!" had so touched Kevin. His sister maybe, she guessed quickly and smiled. "You are so right! You'd think I'd get used to all the hoopla, but somehow, well, tonight is different."

"Yes." The woman nodded. "Because it's Kevin's night."

Suzy got a lump in her throat. "He is something, isn't he?" she said, then her eyes widened. What if this *weren't* his sister? What if . . .

"I—I'm sorry, but we haven't even been introduced. I'm—"

"Oy, do I know who *you* are! You end up in the middle of Kevin's conversations even when we're talking about bagels and lox." The woman laughed a rich throaty laugh that warmed Suzy through to her bones. "I'm Susan Reed. For Kevin I was sort of a mishmash of friend, surrogate mother, and—"

"—and guardian angel!" Kevin broke in. He wrapped an arm around the woman's shoulder and hugged her tight.

She smiled up at him, then winked at Suzy. "You know, I can remember when he wasn't so much bigger than me." She punched him lightly on his broad shoulder. "The kid sort of filled out!"

"All thanks to you and Logan," Kevin signed.

"And the rest of the crew. By the way, where is everyone?"

"I made them promise to wait until at least the mayor had a chance to shake your hand. You know us, once we get ahold of you, no one else stands a chance. Wait, I'll go tell them the coast is clear."

"What a terrific woman," Suzy said to Kevin when Susan had hurried off.

He grinned. "I knew you and she would like each other. And wait till you meet the rest of my family: Logan, the Oasis crew. See, Susan owned a bar and grill, the Waldo Street Oasis. Actually she still owns it, but with six kids and—"

"Six children? She's not terrific, she's amazing!"

"Here we are!" Susan reappeared, her arm looped through that of a tall, handsome man with wheat-colored hair and an easy smile. "This is my husband, Logan. Suzy Keller."

"Happy to meet you, Suzy. And congratulations, Kevin! You deserve it!"

"Mazel tov!" cried a short, plump gray-haired woman. She wrapped Kevin in her arms and patted his back fondly. In a second, a smiling man, also gray-haired, took her place, hugging and patting. Kevin returned the embraces, then flashed another grin. "This, Suzy, is Aunt Blossom and Uncle Buddy. And this"— he reached for a slim Chinese man and pulled him close—"is Stanley Ng." Then he dropped his arm across the broad shoulders of an elderly black man. "And this is Jerome Lewis. Stanley and Jerome are Susan's partners in the bar—"

"Bar and grill!" Susan teased as she had for almost a dozen years now.

"Bar and grill, right!" Kevin laughed, correcting his sign. "And this is Patty Lee, waitress extraordinaire, and her husband, Steve. And that," he finished with a smile, "is my family."

Suzy smiled back into his shining eyes. "Quite the nicest family I've ever met!" she said.

Immediately she was enveloped by their hugs and good wishes, and spent the next few minutes answering their questions and sharing their excitement. Then the crowd, which had been ebbing and receding like a tide, closed in again.

Cocktails were served, and Kevin reached past a young man who was busily jotting notes on a steno pad, and lifted two tulip-shaped glasses of champagne off a tray. He handed one to Suzy, touched it lightly with the rim of his own. and sipped the amber liquid. Suzy raised her glass to her lips and let her eyes smile at him over the rim.

The crowd drew them apart. Talking, smiling, answering hundreds of questions, Suzy found herself on the opposite side of the room from Kevin. Mike had joined him, and they were deep in conversation with the editor of the local business journal.

But, like swimmers separated by a frothing distance of sea, they would often lift their heads and seek the other's face. Their eyes would meet and they'd feel that thrilling, unexpected jolt of connection. Even when someone drew her aside, Suzy could feel Kevin's gaze burning into her bare skin.

He stood there, lean and dark and elegant, set apart from all the others by some power. Did everyone feel it, or just her? Suzy wondered. But yes . . . look at how everyone nodded and agreed with him, hypnotized by him. Even across the room she wasn't safe, she thought helplessly.

As if he felt the heat of that look, Kevin turned to meet her eyes. Desire and arousal surged through his body and he burned within the confines of his tuxedo. Quickly he averted his glance and shook his head to clear it. It must be the night, he thought. The excitement.

But Suzy felt it too! Zing! Pow! It was like the bubbles over the lovers' heads in the comics: wordless, inexplicable. Pure electricity. She had always thought that was make-believe, but here it was, happening to her. She felt her temperature rise and became suddenly, painfully, aware of her body. Her skin tingled and her nipples pressed achingly against the chiffon gown. Tiny dots of perspiration surfaced across the pale rise of her breasts.

She reached for another glass of champagne to cool off and drank it in a few quick gulps. It made her head spin. Actually, the whole world was spinning, a bright pinwheel of colors and sounds. Pressing her fingertips to her throat, she laughed softly. "Pardon me," she said to the mayor's eager young assistant, "but what were you saying?"

Kevin watched Suzy from across the room. He was suddenly, oddly, jealous of that young, grinning kid, of everyone who stood alone with her, talking, laughing. It wasn't just that she was beautiful. No, it was some spell she could weave out of that strange mix of sophistication and naïveté. It touched him the way nothing else ever had. It stole his heart and left him breathless, aching with a desperate desire for something way beyond his reach.

Nodding to Mike, he excused himself and strode briskly across the room. Air, he thought. That was what he needed. Along with a healthy dash of common sense! Where did he get off putting Suzy Keller right smack in the middle of his fantasies? There was no way on earth a perfect woman like that could fit into his life.

He pushed open the balcony door and stepped out into the black night. He had barely taken a deep breath of the warm but refreshing night air when he felt fingers gently touching his arm.

She was there beside him, appearing out of nowhere.

"This is a good idea," she said.

He looked down into her eyes, his hands still.

"You know," she went on, smiling, "I thought you were going to ask me to dance. I mean, that's the way I dreamed it."

"Dreamed it?" he asked, repeating her words carefully in sign.

She blushed. "Yes. I'm saying too much, aren't I? I'm embarrassing you—"

"No!" He paused, then reached out to touch her cheek, only to pull his hand back quickly. "This is the way I dreamed it too," he admitted with a wry grin. "I knew your skin would look like gold. I knew your hair would be a flame." He stopped, narrowing his eyes as if to keep her from seeing into his soul. But something stronger than reason seemed to overtake him and he added softly, "I'm burning anyway."

His hands moved then and wove into the spill of her hair, its color shadowed to russet by the darkness. His fingers grazed the tender nape of her neck, sending shivers of delight racing along her spine. She stood motionless beneath his touch, breathless . . . waiting.

Kevin dropped his hand suddenly, then raised it slowly in careful sign. "Your talk . . . was terrific." He took a deep breath and prayed for calming reason to stay between them.

Suzy nodded a thank-you, emotion flooding her until she didn't trust her voice.

Kevin continued. "You're every—every bit as wonderful as I thought you would be, Suzy." He halted, his hand hovering in midair, then he dropped it slowly to her shoulder. Ross, stop this! a voice in his head rang out. What are you doing? But the voice was dimmed by the beating of his heart, and his fingers moved of their own accord, down and across the pale chiffon. She felt his touch along her shoulder, his cool fingers tracing slowly down across her heated skin until they found the bare, waiting rise of her breasts. She heard the sharp intake of his breath mixed with her own little gasp of surprise and arousal. "Oh, Suzy," he signed. "Suzy, I—"

"I know!" She gave a shaky little laugh that brushed his lips. "I know. I pictured you just like this, all dark and handsome in your tuxedo, looking fierce and tender all at once. And I—I . . ."

"But it's not a dream, Suzy. We can't—"

His signs were lost between their bodies as Suzy, for the first time in her life, found herself unable to speak. Instead, she reached up, pushed her hands into the crisp darkness of his hair, and drew his face down to hers.

His lips brushed across the soft satin of her mouth, a light, questioning touch that sent ripples of pleasure shimmering out across her skin. He lifted her up tightly against him, his lips pressing on hers in a fever of passion that only the cool sweetness of her mouth could quench. She clung to him, arms locked around his neck, letting his body take her weight as she gave herself up to the wonder of their kiss. His tongue rasped across the ripe fullness of her lower lip.

"Kevin, oh, Kevin," she moaned softly, feeling the earth vanish beneath her feet. She knew only the startling happiness of being in his arms. Parting her lips, she touched the tip of her tongue to his, and thrilled to the wild abandon that rose within her as she led his tongue into the sweet cave of her mouth.

Reason screamed, but Kevin's body couldn't hide

his desire. She felt the tightening of his muscles, the wild pounding of his heart. She slipped her hands beneath his jacket and ran them over the solid strength of his body, his heat and power. Dreams do come true, she thought, and a brash little smile tickled at the corner of her mouth.

Kevin felt it and groaned, knowing that another moment and all the reins of self-control would slip from his shaking hands.

With great reluctance he tore his lips away and buried his face in her hair.

Suzy leaned back against the warm circle of his arms. "You never mentioned there were fringe benefits to this job, Mr. Ross," she teased. "But you know, a woman could get used to this. . . ."

He shook his head and gently eased her away. "Not a good idea, Suzy," he signed. "Come on, we've got to get back inside. They may be serving dessert by now." And he needed to get his head back on straight, he thought, although Suzy Keller might have made that impossible!

Tom Hennessey, the president of the Chamber of Commerce, was waiting for them as they stepped back into the room. He halted his pacing midstep and stuck out his hand.

"Congratulations, Kevin. And what a pleasure to meet you, Ms. Keller. You could sell *me* at least a thousand boxes of cookies!" He was all smiles, but Suzy could sense an undercurrent of impatience.

She slipped her hand away from its snug resting place on Kevin's arm and took a step away. "If you gentlemen want to talk business, go right ahead."

Kevin's gaze lingered on her face and Suzy read there exactly what she felt.

She gave a husky little laugh. "Business before

pleasure, Mr. Ross. Besides, I've got to go see if my family has arrived—yet!"

Tom Hennessey smiled wholeheartedly. "Pleasure meeting you, Suzy. Now, Kevin, how about if I grab Mike Pepper and meet you over at the bar in a minute or two? I got a letter from a banker in California who's . . ."

Suzy drifted away from the conversation. She went looking for her family among the crowd and found them surrounded by a small but enthusiastic clutch of reporters. Her mother was holding forth, her father was smiling in that proud paternal way of his, and Nikki was making eyes at a handsome young reporter from *The Star*. He and his colleagues were busy taking notes.

Oh, Mom must be in her glory! Suzy thought, shaking her head in fond amusement. There was nothing Bea Keller liked better than a captive audience, especially when the subject was Suzy's success.

"Yes, our Suzy is a very talented young woman," she was saying now, "as I'm sure most of you know. She is *the* most requested model at the agency, and has been for the last three years. Aren't I correct, Lorraine?"

"One hundred percent true, Bea," the other woman concurred. "And for good reason. She's as bright and charming as she is beautiful. The perfect client, I always say."

"The perfect daughter!" Charles Keller interrupted. "And you people better treat her right, or you'll have to answer to me!" He laughed, only half joking.

"Oh, listen to you all!" Suzy said, slipping between the reporters to give first her mother and then her father a hug.

"Congratulations, Suzy," her father said proudly,

giving her one of his biggest bear hugs as the cameras flashed.

"How about a family portrait?" a photographer asked, and the four of them stood close together, smiling, arms looped around one another's waists.

"I can just see the headlines tomorrow!" Nikki muttered under her breath. 'Famous model, parents . . . and *kid sister* at Kevin's Kookies bash."

Suzy laughed. "I don't think you have a thing to worry about, Nikki. This is Kevin's night. It's *his* picture that will be under the banner headlines tomorrow."

"Nonsense!" her mother scolded. She hated to have the bubble of her illusions pricked, even by her own daughter. A fan of frown lines marred her brow. "Suzy, *you* are the star of his new campaign. Certainly your picture will appear as well." Smiling again, she vamped a wink at the photographers. "And surely you're much more photogenic."

"I'm not so sure about that, Mother," Suzy answered, letting her gaze travel to the incredibly handsome man standing near the bar.

Nikki followed her gaze. "Wow! Is that him? *That's* Kevin?"

"Yes," Suzy said, then smiled. "I told you he was handsome."

"You didn't tell me he was a gorgeous hunk! Oops . . . you're not going to print that, are you?" she asked the reporters, blushing furiously.

Suzy had stopped listening. From across the room Kevin was watching her. She saw the hint of a smile curve his beautiful mouth. One dark brow rose into the lock of hair that always tumbled over his forehead. All of a sudden she was seized with a desire to draw her thumb across that heavy brow. It was as dark as a hawk's wing, and she knew it would feel smooth and silky. And his cheek would be cool, and would rasp slightly against the tender skin of her palm.

Then someone asked Kevin a question and he turned away, releasing her.

Suzy felt as if she had been dropped back to earth without a parachute. Her knees were weak, her pulse fluttering. Pressing her fingertips to her temple, she turned back to her family.

Her mother was watching her, a strange, searching look clouding her eyes. After a moment's silence she said, "So, dear, why don't you tell us a little about this Kevin Ross? I hear he's quite a phenomenon. When we came in, people were all abuzz about the speech you made—"

"And we would have been here to hear it," Charles interrupted, giving his younger daughter a hug, "if your *kid sister* hadn't had to change her clothes ten times."

There, things were back to normal, Suzy thought. She drew a deep breath, trying to relax, then smiled and nodded as the conversation flowed around her. But beneath it all, she was aware of her mother's watchful, appraising stare. Oh, please, she again silently begged, let this go well!

Lorraine and the reporters drifted away and a waiter walked over to them, bringing champagne and hors d'oeuvres.

Jumping into the welcome lull, Suzy told her family about the amazing growth of Kevin's Kookies. She told them the size of the warehouse, the number of deliveries, the interest in franchises, the opening of Kevin's Kookies stores in most of the major malls from Chicago to New York, from Boston to Atlanta. She told it all with great enthusiasm and a wonderful veneer of nonchalance. She told them everything . . . but one thing.

Somehow she never quite found the right moment to mention it. Something in her mother's look, her father's protectiveness, kept her from it. Her parents thought *any* man in her life was cause for concern. She wasn't ready for such things, they would caution wisely and endlessly. Not if she wanted her career. And Suzy had always listened politely and nodded, because it had never mattered before. But now it suddenly mattered so very much.

She snagged another lungful of air and started in again. But the more she talked, the more her throat closed tight, as if those words were stuck there, making everything else hard to say. Silly, she chided herself. You're making a big deal out of nothing.

And all the time she knew he was watching her. Did he know what she was thinking now? Could he read their lips? Did he think she was afraid, or worse, uncomfortable about his deafness? No!

Tossing her hair back from her flushed cheeks, she realized she was trembling. Quickly she hid her hands in the soft folds of her skirt. She dipped her head, hoping to avoid everyone's eyes until she could slow her breathing, steady her pulse. And then she felt the heat of Kevin's gaze on the bare skin of her back. Like a touch, warm and enveloping, it spread through her bones and gave her strength.

She turned and searched the room for him. Like a magnet, his gaze drew hers. He was standing with Mike Pepper, the mayor, and three city councilmen. But when their eyes met, he flashed that heart-stopping smile of his and stepped away.

She smiled back and waved him toward them from across the room. "There," she said to her parents. "He's free now. Good, I want you to meet him." She laughed, a soft, throaty sound full of excitement. "*Nothing* I can tell you is as good as the real thing. Oh, Mom, Dad, I hope you like one another."

"I'm sure we will, dear," her mother said. "Though you seem more concerned than usual about this business relationship. Other times you've kept such a distance. . . ."

"This isn't quite like other times."

"Why not?"

"Of *course* not," her father said, galloping right over the women's words. He dropped an arm across both their shoulders. "This, my darling daughter, is your golden opportunity. Probably the most important thing that has ever happened to you."

"You're right, Dad." Suzy boldly met and held her mother's gaze. "By the way, Kevin's deaf."

"What?" The one word slipped out between Bea's lips.

"How interesting," Charles said, spearing another shrimp from a passing tray.

But when his wife spoke again, her blunt tone caught his full attention. "Suzy dear, I hope you're certainly smart enough not to get involved with this fellow. With *any* fellow," she said. "You are, aren't you, Suzy?"

"But of course she is, dear," Charles said, frowning now. "She has her career ahead of her. She—"

"Mom. Dad. We'll talk about this later."

"I think we should talk about it now," her mother replied, lifting her chin and meeting Kevin's eyes as he strode eagerly toward them.

He knew immediately what had happened. It had happened before, but it had never mattered before. This time it mattered too much.

He froze midstride. His throat went dry, his palms sweaty. His breath burned like fire in his lungs. Forbidding even a trace of pain to cross his face, he grabbed hold of his emotions and shoved them into a tiny box way at the back of his skull.

He knew the truth of what he read in Mrs. Keller's eyes, had known it all along. It was a dream, he thought. Not real, a dream . . . Then why did it hurt so damn much?

He forced his feet to continue moving. And why do you feel like someone has just ripped your heart out? he asked himself. Tough, Ross, but you know all about reality, right? Play the hand as it's dealt.

"Kevin!" Suzy moved to his side and smiled up at him. "This is my father, Charles Keller . . . my mother, Bea. And Nikki. She made me promise not to call her my kid sister!" Her laughter sounded hollow, even to herself.

Her parents were polite but cool. Just as they'd been with every man Suzy had ever brought closer than the photographer's studio. She wanted to shake them, but all she could do was bite her lip.

Kevin shook hands all around, accepting the Kellers' congratulations, their wishes for his continued success. He was polite, pleasant, charming as always. But they were adversaries, facing each other across too high a barrier: his pride, their fear and dismay.

Suzy stood in the middle, translating, fighting back the tears that threatened behind her lids.

"Kevin, how about another quick breath of fresh air?" she asked, slipping her hand around his arm. "I really could use it!"

"I think they're about to serve dinner," he answered, and took his arm away. "You'll be okay."

He looked at her, but it was as if a wall had gone up behind his fierce dark eyes. "And then there will be business talk. Boring, but business is why we're here. Tell them that, Suzy. Tell them that's what this is all about: business."

And he turned on his heel and strode away.

Four

Business, Suzy, that's what this is all about. . . .
In the hectic week that followed, Suzy tried out the words in every possible way, said them aloud and silently, in sign and in the middle of a restless sleep. And no way, *ever,* did they fit. And when she was finally able to corner Kevin Ross, she'd certainly let him know it!

And maybe, just maybe, today would be that day, she thought, as she readied herself for the photographers.

"Charlotte, where is Gallos?" The tall, thin man took a long drag on his cigarette and strutted angrily over to a woman holding a stenographer's tablet.

"Don't worry, Edward, he'll be here. He needed to pick up some extra lighting."

"And the girl?"

"She's been here for an hour."

Edward registered disbelief, then followed the woman's pointing finger. "Oh, my. What a beauty! And prompt to boot."

51

The woman raised her head and stared at the photographer for a moment, then retorted, "Professional, Ed, that's all. And fairly calm," she mumbled to the pad as she resumed her note-making, "unlike some people I know."

In a corner of the large studio Suzy sat on a pile of pillows with her face carefully made up and a terry-cloth robe wrapped around her. She sat with a model's stillness, a thick book closed and ignored on her lap, and watched each new arrival with a hopeful glimmer in her emerald eyes.

Surely Kevin would come for the shooting, she thought. He'd been so involved in the PR company's plans, had so much invested in it. Once these photos were shot and ready to go, the advertising campaign would begin in earnest. A "blitz," the PR man called it. There'd be talk shows, billboards, newspaper stories, magazine articles. Her head swam with the schedule that had been laid out for her. But she could do it. She never questioned that!

A small frown creased her forehead. Her emotions were more of a concern right now than any schedule had ever been. Was there any way to keep Kevin Ross out of her mind?

She needed time to be with him, to talk to him. She'd felt so close to him, and then . . . poof! After the party he began treating her just as he treated everyone else, with a cool smile and a wave from a distance. Surely he hadn't let her parents' coolness bother him? *Kevin?* She dismissed the thought with a flick of her fingers. His character tended toward arrogance, boldness. It was unlikely that he'd let her parents keep him from what he wanted. Unless . . . unless he had decided he didn't *want* there to be anything between them.

She gulped air as a wave of misery washed over

her. Had she seemed naïve, too much her parents' "little girl"? Maybe she *had* let them influence her for too long, but her career had tied them all so tightly together. . . .

Her brows drew together in a determined frown and she tapped one tapered nail on the book. Well, setbacks were a part of life. They didn't scare Suzy Keller off, not one whit!

"Suzy, there you are." Mike Pepper strode over and grinned down at her. "Wow! You look gorgeous! And not half as nervous as *I* feel. Say, where's Kevin?"

Suzy gracefully drew herself up from the pillows and shook her head. With a wistfulness that caused Mike a pang of jealousy, she said, "I've been wondering the same thing, Mike. He *will* come, won't he?"

"Sure." Mike stuck his hands into the pockets of his slacks and laughed. "That guy's too pigheaded to let anyone else make decisions—at least not without his okay. He'll be here. But you probably ought to get ready for the first series of shots in the meantime."

Suzy nodded in agreement and walked off to the dressing room.

Someone helped her slip into a yellow and white gingham dress with a full, flowing skirt edged in lace, and an off-the-shoulder neckline. The hairdresser tugged her bright hair up into the inevitable ponytail and fluffed her bangs. The makeup man dusted sheer powder across her shoulders, enough to avoid the glare of the lights without hiding the constellation of freckles that trailed across her skin.

There she was: the girl next door. The girl you'd want to invite over for cookies and milk, while any red-blooded man would be dreaming of kissing the last crumbs off her lips.

"Magnificent!" Edward proclaimed, poking his head out from behind the camera when she reappeared. "You are perfect, darling! Now up, up—" He flapped the air and motioned her onto the raised platform.

Suzy settled herself on the white couch, which in turn was set against a pristine white background. She looked around and laughed. It was just like the kitchen at the cookie factory, a floury white cloud!

Edward snapped the camera. "Incredible smile, Suzanne!"

"Suzy," she corrected him with a grin, and he snapped again.

"Whatever, darling. That back light, Gallos? Change the angle, please, and . . . there we are!"

Regular as a heartbeat, the camera clicked.

"Think cookie!" Edward intoned, and Suzy laughed aloud. She'd been told to think Bahamas, the Mediterranean, blue skies and star-studded nights, her first delicious romance—but never cookies! Yet cookies made her think of Kevin . . . and Kevin made her think of all the others.

From behind the collection of cameramen and assistants and equipment, beyond the glaring lights that focused brightly on Suzy, Kevin slipped almost unnoticed into the room. He stood there silently, his heart hammering beneath his ribs. Oh, but she took his breath away! It was almost animallike, this feeling that gripped him and tore at him so ruthlessly. He cursed it and savored it at once, half mad with wanting and needing her. He couldn't eat, couldn't sleep. With the back of his hand he wiped the sweat from his brow, then raked his fingers through his hair. His breath was a harsh rasp in his throat, and even his clothes felt tight, strangling him. Maybe the Kansas City heat had finally addled his brain!

At that moment Suzy turned and looked right at him, her head tipped back as if to catch an invisible wash of sunlight.

Time stopped for that brief moment. Kevin felt the electric zing of contact as their eyes met. He couldn't have moved if he wanted to, his body transfixed by a wild jolt of desire. Then Suzy had to turn away for a different pose, and he breathed again and stumbled away.

He bumped into Mike at the door.

"Hey, when did you get here, buddy?" Mike asked. "Isn't she something! The camera loves her, and TV's going to love her, and the entire cookie-eating public—" He broke off, looking curiously at Kevin. "Are you okay?"

Kevin tore his gaze away from Suzy and nodded once to Mike, then turned abruptly and stalked out of the room.

Mike caught up with him at the end of the polished empty hallway.

"What's up?" Mike asked. "You're acting mighty strange for an almost mogul. You should be haughty, proud . . . you know, act like a VIP," he joked, but Kevin's response was nonexistent and Mike saw the muscles jump along his friend's set jaw.

"Sorry, Kevin, just a feeble attempt to cheer you up. What's bothering you? The shooting is going great guns. Suzy's a natural—a cookie gal to beat all cookie gals!"

Kevin nodded, glowering. What could he say? he wondered. How could he explain without sounding like a sunfried idiot? She *was* perfect, dammit! He filled his lungs with air, let it out slowly, then met Mike's puzzled look. "Fire her, Mike," he signed, the heaviness of his thoughts making his hands awkward.

"What? You're crazy!"

Kevin nodded. "Maybe, but do it *now*."

"No!" Mike stood his ground and stared at his friend. Sometimes Ross was a lawyer's nightmare, he thought. A sure thing sitting comfortably in the palm of his hand, and he wanted to throw it away. "No, Kevin, I won't let you. Why in hell would you want to do that?"

"Because, Mike, she's driving me crazy. I'm horny as hell every time she comes near me!"

Mike's low, rumbling laughter echoed off the painted walls. With great relief he slapped his friend on the back. "You need to let loose, buddy. There are far wiser ways of taking care of that problem than firing Suzy Keller!"

Kevin gave him one threatening glare and strode away.

Alone in a darkened bar in Westport, just a few blocks from the Oasis, Kevin sat and nursed his third beer of the afternoon, hoping to be left alone with his misery. His strong, blunt fingers thrummed along the polished surface of the bar.

"Hey, there," the elderly bartender said, winking. "Doncha tell me Kevin Ross has a problem! Our famous boy wonder?" He reached over the bar top and ruffled Kevin's hair affectionately. They all knew Kevin down here, all liked him, all celebrated his success.

Kevin forced a half-smile and shrugged.

"Only thing makes a fella look like you look, Kevin, is women! They'll do it every time." Ernie brushed a few thin gray hairs off his forehead and looked around at the gathering happy-hour crowd. "Yep, Kevin, that's it. They can put a smile on your face"—his eyes twinkled mischievously—"but they sure as hell can take it away!" He gave a friendly wave to a curvy blonde, who immediately came over and lifted herself onto the barstool next to Kevin's.

"Hi, Kevin, Ernie. What's up?" She pressed against the edge of the bar as she turned toward Kevin, and her summery T-shirt pulled taut as intended across her ample, braless breasts.

"Hi, Annie," Kevin signed, then reached for his beer. Damn, he wished she wouldn't get so close. Her breasts brushed his arm and he stiffened. This wasn't helping at all—Annie didn't have anything that could cool the flames Suzy had lit. Tossing back his head, he downed the rest of his beer and signaled for another.

"Summer blues, Kev?" Annie asked. She rubbed one long, painted nail up and down his arm and Kevin watched as his skin responded to her touch. He shook his head. Annie was a nice kid. Always wanted everybody to feel good. And in her free spirited, simple-hearted way, she'd be happy to do *whatever* she could to make Kevin smile.

"It's too hot," he signed noncommittally.

"You've been ignoring us, Kev. Haven't seen you here for a while."

"Been busy, Annie. Making money takes a lot of time." He gave her an offhanded grin.

"Even so, Kev, don't forget your friends!" Her fingers wound around his upper arm and squeezed with light, teasing pressure.

Forgetting his beer, he stood abruptly and wrapped one arm around her shoulders, signing with his free hand. "Sorry, babe, it's not you. Old Kevin needs a wall to hit."

He kissed her lightly on the top of her head and walked out into the fading daylight, leaving a very disappointed blonde staring at the door behind him.

• • •

In memory, he could see the small dark-haired boy he had been moving in the shadows, walking alone down a neighborhood street dotted with kids who stared and pointed. They were of another world, not his world, no matter how badly he wanted it. And he'd *never* let them know just how badly he did want it. *Foster kid*, they shouted, standing in their little group. *Dumb foster kid! Weirdo.* And Kevin would fight them. All of them. Or they'd run away and he'd be left with his unbearable anger. Then he'd find a dark alley and a tough stick. He'd hit out at everything, and let escape the words he'd never utter in front of anyone. He'd slash the stick at bushes and trash cans and fences and walls, feeling the anger and frustration flow out through the piece of wood clenched in his hand.

But he also could remember *before* deafness, could remember the world of sound. The whistling of the wind through the trees, and music, and the words to games. And voices: his mother's voice . . . and his own, loud with the energy of any five-year-old boy.

Then that world had been snatched away, and there had been no one who cared enough to help him reach it again.

But now things were different. Kevin shoved his hands deeper into his pockets and walked faster down the crowded street. Now he had friends, money, success—he had the world. He should feel contentment, not this nagging restlessness chewing away at his insides.

Trouble is, Ross, he told himself, you want something again, something you damn well can't have.

He wanted Suzy Keller. Wanted her with that same painful fierceness he'd felt in his childhood. He wanted to touch her, to run his hands over the soft curves of her hips and lift her high into the air. Wanted to feel the weight of her body against his own and to smell her tantalizing odors. He wanted to love her. He wanted her to love him!

A harsh laugh escaped his lips. All those irrational "wants," desires that couldn't be fulfilled. Suzy was perfect—with incredible opportunities flung before her, stretching out as long as a lifetime. A perfect, beautiful dream woman. How could she ever love *him*? A deaf man could *never* capture a Suzy Keller and fill her needs.

With a bang that turned heads, Kevin pushed his way through the health club doors. In minutes he appeared alone on the polished racquetball court. The stick of his childhood had been replaced by a racket, and there was a ball now instead of trash cans. But the pain of not-having was as real as the sharp, echoing anger that bounced off the walls and ceiling and floor, and the sweat that poured out of him, making dark, widening splotches on his T-shirt. He could *hear* the sharp smack of the ball on the walls, the rebound and retort of it in the enclosed space. He could hear it, could feel it in his gut; could feel the jarring impact travel up his arm and across his shoulders and chest; could feel his breath burn in his lungs, his muscles burn in his legs.

He played until he couldn't move, then stood there, bent at the waist, his hands on his thighs, his back heaving with ragged breaths.

Enough! his body begged, and finally the image of her in his head was blurred by exhaustion. Then he quit, hung the towel around his neck, and staggered back to the locker room. The sauna eased his sore muscles and the shower washed away the taste and smell of physical exertion and anger, and soon Kevin felt in control again. He walked back out into the Kansas City dusk and threw his head back to catch the faint traces of a breeze. Kevin Ross was a survivor. He'd handled more difficult things . . . hadn't he?

And then he stopped still. It was strange the way he knew she was there before he even saw her. A feeling, a movement of air, perhaps? Or maybe it was her wonderful fresh scent that he had already come to anticipate and delight in.

She was sitting on a stone wall a short distance from the health club entrance, her long, slender legs swinging loosely, her fiery hair silhouetted against the last fading traces of daylight.

Kevin paused in the middle of the sidewalk and their gazes closed the distance between them. Suzy broke the silence, her voice a whisper as she signed hesitantly, "Didn't you like the way the session was going?"

She looked so young in her jeans and loose-fitting blouse, her face rubbed clean of the modeling makeup. He wanted to race to her and scoop her up, hold her tightly in his arms.

Instead, he half-smiled and shook his head. "You were beautiful," he signed.

"Then why?" she insisted. "Why did you walk out like that? So suddenly, without a word?"

"How did you find me?" he asked, avoiding her questions. He walked slowly over to where she sat and swung his body up easily beside hers.

"Simple. Mike sent me to Ernie at the bar, and Ernie and a pretty blond girl suggested I look here." She laughed and lifted one shoulder lightly. "Is she a friend?"

Kevin drew his brows together in puzzlement.

"The pretty blonde—she seemed to know you well." Her hands moved slowly and carefully.

He smiled. "That's just Annie; she's a nice kid."

"How nice?"

He watched the shadows play across her lovely face and squeezed his hand into a tight fist to keep from tracing the line of her cheekbones. Finally he released his fingers and signed slowly. "So . . . how did the shooting go?"

"Kevin!" Suzy bristled and lifted her hand to his cheek to turn his face toward hers. "You're avoiding all my questions!"

He forced himself to focus on her words. "Sorry. What was it you asked?"

She shook her head and laughed. "Okay, I'll try another topic. It's time we got better acquainted. I want to know more about you, Kevin. I know the little you told me for the speech, but how in heaven's name did you ever start a cookie factory?"

He watched her closely. Her face was so open, so refreshing! It was true; they did know very little about each other, yet there were no uncomfortable pauses, none of the hasty excuses that he had long ago learned to expect from strangers. Suzy Keller was a whole new surprise!

"Okay, Suzy, you asked for it." He slid down off the wall and looked back up at her. "But not without food. Be back in a minute."

He returned before she could count her good fortune—she had been ready for a much tougher fight to claim his time!—and Suzy shifted on the stone wall to make room for the container of spiced shrimp and the two cold beers Kevin carefully set down.

"There." He lifted himself back up beside her and leaned against a tree that offered its broad trunk to both of them. "Now, Suzy Keller, we're ready." Damn, it felt good. Sharing, talking, sitting with someone who wanted to listen. And what could it hurt? An innocent, friendly conversation, nothing more, nothing less.

Suzy opened the box of shrimp and sighed in delight as she pulled one out by the tail. "Mmmm! Your story is going to have to be pretty good to top these shrimp!" She savored the piece of spicy seafood, then lifted one brow. "Okay, Kevin, shoot. Tell me about you, about your friends the Reeds. I *really* liked them. Have you known them long?"

He smiled slowly, took a long swig of beer, and began, pulling Suzy back through the long years, back to the day he met Susan Rosten Reed. It was a mind-journey he'd never taken anyone on before.

"I was going through a rough time," he told her. "I was about eighteen, on my own on the streets, and Logan patched up my hand when I slammed it none too nicely through a display case in a bakery. And Susan kept me from going back to the streets. She gave me a job in her bar and grill, a bed in the back room, and a future. No one else had ever cared."

Suzy watched carefully, the shrimp forgotten as his sign slowed and his face mirrored the emotion that filled his heart.

"We were all a crazy family back then: Susan and Logan—they weren't married when I met them—Stanley the bartender and Jerome the cook. And Patty Lee, who had her first baby right in the middle of the bar one day!" As he spelled their names, his eyes sparkled at the happy flow of memory. "Susan already knew sign, and the others all learned, even Susan's aunt and uncle, Blossom and Buddy. They shared their lives with me, taught me everything they knew, helped me become a man instead of a scared kid. They made up for everything that happened before." He grinned. "And they fell in love with the cookies I made in the back kitchen!"

"And Kevin's Kookies were born?"

"Not quite so quickly. First we just sold them in the bar. Then a banker who hung out at the Oasis decided they were good enough to invest in.

So he did, along with Logan and Susan and others."

"And you did all this, you came from nothing . . . to this? Kevin!" She seemed about to fling her arms around him, and he held up his hands to stop her.

"Hey, wait! I like being Superman to you, Suzy, but I'm really not. It took luck, hard work, good friends. Without them, I'd still be back punching people's windows out. I'd still be filled with anger, floundering . . ."

"Maybe, maybe not, Kevin. *I* think you're remarkable. And you'll never change my mind about that." Her eyes were round as saucers as she gazed into his. Her voice grew soft. "Kevin?"

"Yes, Suzy?"

"Your deafness . . . was it from birth?"

He shook his head and pain flashed behind his dark eyes at the memory. "Five. I was five. There was an accident. My mom wasn't married, just some poor kid herself, and things must have been tough for her. One day she drove the car off a bridge."

"Oh, Kevin—" Her hand flew to her mouth.

"She died. I had a head injury. It left me like this. Deaf." He touched his ear, then closed his hands in front of him. His signs were short and clipped. Painful.

Suzy leaned against him, resting her head in the angle between his chin and shoulder.

Kevin tensed, then breathed in and out slowly as he tried to calm the beating of his heart. There was nowhere for his arm to go but around her back, gently supporting her weight against his body.

When both their hearts had stilled, Suzy looked up at him again. "But that means you *did* hear. . . ."

"Yes. Once, a lifetime ago."

"And nothing could be done?"

"No. There was nerve damage. And I didn't have anyone even if there had been a way. I was on the streets or in and out of foster homes, and the foster parents couldn't cope with the handicap."

"*They* couldn't handle it. What about *you*?" The sudden anger at people she'd never met exploded inside Suzy, and her slender body shook beneath his arm.

"That's life, Suzy." He shrugged and tightened his grip on her shoulder.

"No, that's inhumanity!"

"Well, I survived."

She looked up at him, her eyes searching his dear, handsome face. "It must have been awful." Her hair brushed against his cheek and she pressed closer, feeling the strong beat of his heart.

"What was awful was not having anyone who gave a damn, who would help me reach the world that I'd been jerked out of. I couldn't do it alone."

· "No, no, you couldn't," Suzy murmured softly, only the feel of her words noticed by Kevin as they swept over his bare neck.

"I resented that for a long time, I guess. So I stopped trying to talk and everyone seemed relieved somehow."

"You were so alone," she whispered, and thought of her own family, of her sheltered life and a home that was filled to overflowing with love that cushioned and nurtured her. Her throat tightened and she could feel the hot tears gathering behind her lids.

"Hey, don't cry," he signed, brushing his fingers gently across her cheeks. "Please, it's all over. It was a long time ago."

"But it's so unfair. You had nothing. No one. And all my life I've had this wonderful family and this beautiful home and . . ."

"I'm glad. I couldn't stand to think of you unhappy. Or scared." He placed his palm against the curve of her cheek and tipped her face up to his. Smiling, he kissed the tip of her nose. "Enough of this hearts and flowers stuff. Tell me about *your* family. They seem . . . like nice people."

A frown wrinkled her brow at the frustrating memory of his one and only encounter with her parents. She nodded fervently. "They *are*, Kevin. And I hope you'll give them another chance to prove it."

He shook his head, his lips set in a straight line. "They don't have to *prove* anything—"

"Oh, yes, they do! But as stubborn and conservative as they are, they are also very kind and loving."

"And very proud of their daughter. And concerned about her career."

Suzy saw the smile of understanding in his eyes, but beneath it there was a faint flicker of hurt.

"Yes, I know, I know!" She smiled back. "They're very protective. Any man is a threat to my career, they think."

"*Any* man?"

"Oh, yes. Mom has ingenious ways of making men see that I'd really be a bad bet." She laughed. "But that's just Mom. And her heart is in the right place, even though it's hard to understand her pride sometimes. Do you know she even *named* me after a famous model? Ten minutes old and they had plans for me!"

Kevin smiled, half-listening, his mind lingering on her earlier words. "Any man" was a threat. Then how much more a threat would be a deaf man! His gaze shifted to her lovely face and her long, graceful hands as she formed the words, and he forced himself to focus on what she was saying.

"It's true. They named me for Suzy Parker. I heard about Suzy Parker from the time I was old enough to walk!"

"Well, I know you are every bit as fine and beautiful."

"Ha!" Suzy threw her hands up in the air. "Another one!" Then she grew serious and looked into his face. "No, I'll never be Suzy Parker."

"What will you be?" he asked softly.

She cocked her head to one side and looked beyond Kevin's shoulders to the stars just beginning to twinkle in the distance. "Many different things, I think. I *do* want to succeed at modeling. That isn't just my parents' dream. But I'm not sure exactly where I want that modeling to take me."

"I think it could take you far. You could be famous . . . an international beauty."

"Maybe," was all she said, looking deep into his shadowed eyes.

He kept signing, glad he didn't have to talk around the sudden tightness in his throat. "This will be a good start for you then. The cookie campaign will give you a lot of national exposure. Magazines. TV."

She nodded in agreement, a slow, sexy smile lighting her face. "Oh, Mr. Ross, I expect to get a lot out of the cookie campaign." One slim hand settled firmly on his thigh.

Kevin felt the fire leap through him, centered hotly in his loins. "Suzy, I . . ."

"Yes, Kevin?" She tipped her face back, her fingers circling slowly on the tight denim of his jeans. A wisp of a breeze sailed by them unnoticed.

"I . . ." His hand lingered between them for just a second, his fingers still speaking the single word.

He could feel the heat of her breasts just a whisper away. Gradually the tightness fell from his hand and his fingers loosened, then moved to cradle her shoulder. His hand slipped automatically into the silken waves of her hair. Cupping her chin with the other hand, he looked deeply into the emerald eyes that never wavered, never blinked away the message that lay there.

And slowly but inexorably Kevin's lips came down to meet hers in a kiss Suzy had been waiting for for days.

You're dreaming! Kevin's mind told him. Don't do this. . . . But the excitement racing through his eager body told him differently. The sweet pressure of her lips on his was very, very real. Gently at first, then with a rising hunger he could no longer suppress, he sought to explore the sweetness of her mouth. A haze of sensations swirled about him: the clean, tantalizing scent of her, the heat of their bodies, the stillness of the darkening summer night. With a sureness born of desire, he slowly traced the outline of her parted lips with his tongue, then slipped inside to taste the honey he knew was waiting there.

Suzy's breath stopped. The world stood still and the heavenly darkness didn't go away when she opened her eyes. Snatching a quick lungful of air, she pressed closer to Kevin, her breasts rubbing against his chest, her hands traveling across his broad shoulders and into the wonderful thick hair at his neck. "Oh, Kevin," she murmured as she claimed his lips again, returning the soft, sensuous welcome of his kiss.

They were side by side now, pressed tightly together on the old brick wall. Young lovers to the dark world beyond, heavenly explorers to each other. Kevin's hand dropped until his fingers brushed the firm curve of her breasts and his mind played with the thought of what lay just beneath his fingertips. In slow, dreamlike movements, he traced the perfect contours of her body through the thin cotton of her shirt until the moan that escaped her lips swept across his cheeks like a summer breeze.

"Kevin . . ." She curled his hair around her fingers.

He could taste his name on her lips. He felt the wild flutter of her heart beating against his chest, and the fierce pleasure pulsing through his body.

Suzy drew her face away but an inch, putting her fingers where her lips had been. Watching him, she traced the outline of his generous mouth, laughing when he nipped playfully at her fingertips. This felt so right, so *fated* . . . as inevitable as rain in spring, she mused dreamily, her eyes slowly closing, her thick lashes brushing her flushed cheeks.

He kissed both lids, then buried his face in her hair, his warm breath sending shivers across her skin. With great effort he pulled himself away. "Suzy," he asked, "what's happening here?"

She looked lovingly into his eyes. What was happening here? she repeated silently. She lifted her hand between them and moved her index finger slowly. "You . . . me . . ."

Kevin's gaze fell to her hand. How could signs be so sexy? But Suzy's were, sexy and sensual, languid and loving. He took a deep breath and moved slightly away. It was clear Suzy wasn't going to slow things down here. "Suzy."

"Yes, Kevin?" She shifted her body to stay pressed tight against his side.

Kevin drew a breath between clenched teeth and held it, fighting an overwhelming urge to leap off the brick wall and carry her through the night to his bed. It was what every throbbing nerve in his body was demanding. And then what? Roll over and call it a night? Or have a short, heated affair as they tried to get the campaign off the ground? And when the inevitable happened, when Suzy went on with her life, her career, then what? Shake hands and say good-bye?

It couldn't be like that with Suzy; he knew that already. Once she was a part of his life, he wouldn't ever forget her. But he knew just as clearly that their lives couldn't ever become one. Suzy Keller deserved a damn sight more than a deaf cookie maker!

None of his thoughts ran smoothly through his head. They all had jagged, painful edges. Suzy didn't fit in those thoughts. Not in his life. Not Suzy Keller . . .

Kevin groaned and wedged the box of shrimp between them. He ran one finger down the side of her cheek, relishing the starlight in her eyes, then looked away. "Suzy, eat a shrimp. Please!"

Five

It wasn't the spiced shrimp Suzy remembered from her Friday night on the stone wall, nor was it seafood she thought about as she posed before Edward's ever-present camera, or savored as she stood beneath the beating spray of the shower. It was Kevin. Always Kevin. And she knew she'd somehow have to break through the reserve he seemed to pull up out of thin air.

Attack him on the loading dock? Send him gifts from a secret admirer? Be more assertive? Suzy ticked off playful alternatives as she waltzed down the hall of the warehouse several days later.

"Hi, Ethel!" she said as she breezed into the secretary's office and paused at the edge of the cluttered desk. "Is Kevin busy? I didn't want to just barge in."

"Oh, he's busy all right, Suzy. He and Mike are poring over plans." She waved her hands in the air. "Things are getting really crazy around here, you know? The phones don't stop for love nor money, the newspapers call, radio . . ."

Suzy laughed. "Terrific, huh?"

"Absolutely! Never in my wildest dreams did I think it would go this far."

Suzy shook her finger in mock reprimand. "How could you have doubted Kevin Ross, Ethel? That man could walk on water, move mountains!"

Ethel laughed at the unabashed enthusiasm on Suzy's face. "And so could you, Suzy, dear!"

"Think so, Ethel?" Suzy dropped her voice and whispered conspiratorily, "Think I can move Kevin Ross?"

Ethel laughed at the sexy smile that spread across Suzy's face. "If anyone can, Suzy, it will be you. Go on in. I know he'll be glad to see you."

Suzy grinned and marched down to Kevin's office. She flung open the door and called, "Hi, everyone!"

Kevin's back was to the door and only Mike looked up from the table where the two men were studying huge sheets of paper. "Suzy, hi!"

She put a finger to her lips and walked over to the back of Kevin's chair. While Mike looked on in amusement, she leaned over and covered Kevin's eyes with her hands.

He reached up and firmly grasped her hands in his own. He wasn't surprised at all. There wasn't any way Suzy Keller could hide her presence from him anymore. When she walked into a room, he knew it instantly. He knew he had felt her even before Mike had heard her. Every inch of his body reacted to the sudden electricity in the air. Now he lowered her hands and swung her around to the side of the chair.

She leaned against the armrest and grinned. "Hi! Thought I'd better stop in and check on you two. See if you were doing your job. You know, see if you needed me . . ."

Kevin shifted in the chair as the familiar stirrings awoke inside of him. Need her? If she only knew!

"Your timing is perfect, Suzy," Mike said. "We

just got the proofs back from the first shooting. Look." He shifted some papers, pulled out a pile of glossies, and held them out to her.

Suzy looked at Kevin before taking the photos.

"They're great," he signed, surprised by the flash of nervousness in her wide eyes.

She slipped down into a chair and carefully scrutinized each photo. "Yes, yes, these are nice," she said frankly. "But I think that the casual shots Edward took yesterday are going to be the real key." She grinned at Kevin. "Wearing that chef's hat was a stroke of genius, Kevin! And the shots taken with the cooks over by the ovens were great! Flour everywhere . . . and the workers were terrific. You'd think they'd been modeling all their lives."

Kevin smiled, enjoying the energy she radiated. Hot enough to melt steel. "You charmed them."

It had been Suzy's idea to do the kitchen shots. She'd donned her form-fitting jeans and a bright green Kevin's Kookies T-shirt and charmed every last employee as well as the cameramen. Even old die-hard Harry Wilson, the head cook, had grinned and struck a pose with Suzy licking the cookie dough off a long-handled spoon.

Who could resist her? She whirled through the factory each day, red hair flying, dancing through the hallways and kitchen and packing rooms, signing to everyone. She was a bright flame that drew people like helpless moths.

And Suzy made keeping a distance from her about as easy as not thinking about her! She was the most affectionate woman he'd ever met, always touching his arm, hugging him in appreciation, settling her hand on his leg while they talked. He might have claimed it was the humid August weather, but it was really Suzy Keller who was driving him to cold showers five times a day.

He flexed the muscles across his broad back

and tried a casual shrug. "I'm glad you're pleased with the way things are going."

"Now," Suzy went on, "since we have the long Labor Day weekend ahead of us, I thought maybe we could take some extra time and you could teach me more details about how the company works." She smiled boldly into Kevin's face.

Mike laughed. "I think I'll bow out here. *My* weekend is going to be spent with a beautiful brunette down at the Lake of the Ozarks. And we're not taking a single book or plan—or cookie!—with us."

"Mike!" Suzy scolded. "Where's your dedication?"

"Waiting for me at her apartment." He winked and disappeared through the doorway.

Suzy turned her attention back to Kevin. "Well, what do you say, boss? Do you have any time to spare?"

Kevin leaned back in the chair and watched her carefully. What the hell was she doing to him? "Well, Suzy," he signed carefully, "it's kind of a busy weekend. I'm meeting with the investors tomorrow . . . then I have this picnic—"

"Picnic?" Her face lit up. "I love picnics!"

He coughed, then broke into laughter. What was a guy to do? "Want to come?"

"I'd love to! Thanks, Kevin!" She leaned over and hugged him enthusiastically. "Who, what, where?"

"It's an annual event. A celebration of all our 'labor'—from Susan's bar's beginnings, to Patty Lee in the Oasis, to my cookie factory. Susan and Logan have it at their house since they have so much room, and all our old friends will be there with their kids, dogs . . . the whole works."

"It sounds wonderful! I'll bring my famous chocolate cake and call Susan tonight to see what else she might need. And my football, of course, and—"

"Football? You?"

She stood and pushed her fists into her hips, striking an offended pose. "Yes, me! Problems with that, Ross? I'm pretty terrific as a linebacker."

He hooted and signed with skepticism, "Well, it *is* the Show-Me State, Suzy."

"And I definitely will!" She hugged him tightly and disappeared.

"Oh, Suzy . . ." The sign was long and slow and dramatic, drawn out like a lazy wolf whistle. "Where, oh, where would the K.C. Chiefs be if they had had you?"

Suzy hopped into the van with KEVIN'S KOOKIES blockprinted on the sides and laughed lightly. "Super Bowl, most likely!" She glanced down at the brilliant blue football jersey that covered her with a teasing tightness. "A high school beau gave it to me years ago and wouldn't take it back after we stopped going steady. He was a little guy."

Kevin's laughter rumbled through the van. "I believe it."

"Okay, boss, where do Susan and Logan live?"

"Not too far." Kevin pulled the van from the curb and headed south and across the state line to Kansas. It didn't take long before they had left the busyness of the city and suburbs behind them and the highway was bordered by rolling wheat fields and rambling houses silhouetted against the clear blue sky.

"Ah, country folks," Suzy said. She tapped Kevin on the shoulder, then repeated it as he looked at her.

He nodded and with one hand explained, "They moved here when the twins were born. Logan's a doctor and this place is a bit far from the hospital, but they love the quiet."

Suzy nodded thoughtfully as she mused over what he had said. *Love the quiet.* Kevin lived in quiet all the time. How did *he* feel about quiet? How did he feel about relationships? How did he feel about *her*? The green fields swept by unnoticed. She was lost in thought, in the powerful emotions this dark-eyed, handsome man evoked in her.

About thirty minutes later Kevin turned off the highway through white picket gates and drove up a long, circular drive that led to a rambling white two-story house bursting with color and activity. He parked the van alongside several cars and faced Suzy.

"Ready for this?" he asked.

Her brows shot up into her bangs. "Sure. It's going to be great!"

"Great. Right. But a lot different from seeing each other over business. Lots of friends, lots of family." He shrugged, rubbing one hand across his jaw. He wasn't at all sure *he* was ready! Business at least was safe. Neutral ground. But here . . .

"Of course it will be different," Suzy said. She laughed, tossing her hair like a frisky colt. "Besides, I already know Susan and Logan from the cocktail party. And"—she squeezed his thigh in the way that made his blood race—"any friend of yours is a friend of mine!"

"Suzy!" Susan appeared at the side of the van and pulled the door open. "Welcome to our home. We're so happy you could come."

Suzy hopped out, balancing a large cardboard box in her hands as she did so. "Thanks, Susan. Here's the cake. What a beautiful place you have!"

Susan beamed. "It's home."

"To all of us!" Kevin added, and Susan's smile broadened at the compliment.

"Suzy, dear!"

Suzy spun around on the gravel drive, nearly dropping the chocolate cake on Susan's toes.

"Mother!"

Bea Keller tentatively approached the small group, her palms running up and down the soft linen of her slacks. "We're a—a surprise, dear. Your father and sister are here also." Bea hugged Suzy tightly, then pulled away and smiled softly at her daughter, who looked so very radiant.

"And what about Great-Aunt Ruth from Escanaba?" Suzy joked in bewildered amazement.

"It was spur-of-the-moment," Susan explained. "Logan ran into your father at a meeting and we thought it would be nice."

"Susan is a dear," Bea said, then slowly, finally, turned around completely and faced Kevin.

As she watched, Suzy noted that her mother's smile stayed carefully in place, as if moving it might somehow make it disappear completely. But when Bea spoke, her voice was quietly genuine.

"I thought . . . that is, *we* decided after Logan kindly invited us, that it would be a nice time to get to know you better, Kevin, as well as the Reeds."

Suzy's surprise melted into a loving smile. "Well, I—I think that's a good idea, Mother." She looked from one to the other, then tucked the chocolate cake into her mother's arms. "A terrific idea, in fact! And for starters, maybe Kevin can show you where the kitchen is." She grinned, then gave her mother a gentle push.

Smiling, Kevin stepped in and rescued the cake from Bea's grasp. Suzy watched with delight as the smile that made her pulse race tugged gently at her mother's reserve.

Kevin gestured to the rambling house beyond and Bea nodded hesitatingly, then matched her step to his and walked up the path beside him.

"Now, Suzy," Susan began as Kevin and Bea

walked out of earshot, "I want you to feel at home here. The place is yours. There's a fishing pond, horses, whatever."

Suzy smiled, but her eyes sought out Kevin as he disappeared into the house.

Susan followed her gaze. All Suzy Keller wanted was Kevin, she realized. She turned back to Suzy and spoke softly. "We were awfully glad Kevin brought you out today. He's very special to us, you should know."

Suzy read Susan's message easily. Special. We care about him. *Don't hurt him.*

"He's special to me, too, Susan. Very special. I think Kevin Ross is one of the most intriguing, wonderful men I've ever met."

Susan nodded as she watched the sparkle in the young woman's eyes and thought back to the time she'd fallen head over heels in love with Logan Reed. Had she looked like that? she wondered. Soft and vulnerable and a little bit cloudy? Because that was exactly what Suzy Keller was doing. She was falling head over heels in love with Kevin. "So, you like our Kevin. Good. Then you'll work well together."

Suzy's laughter punctuated the gentle game-playing. "Yes, Susan. *Very* well." Then Suzy grew serious and gazed searchingly at Susan. "I know how much Kevin means to you and Logan. And you to him. He's told me a little about his past . . ."

Susan's dark brows rose slightly, but she held her silence. She knew Kevin didn't talk easily about his past.

"I also realize you don't know me from Adam, but you're a very sensitive, perceptive woman, so you must know that I'm crazy about Kevin, and *not* because it's his name on my paycheck!"

Susan's husky laughter eased the tension and

she tucked her arm into the lovely redhead's. "I like you, Suzy. I think we understand each other."

Suzy smiled, but a nagging little worry nibbled at her heart. "Is there a 'but' on the end of that sentence, Susan?"

Susan paused and chose her words carefully. "Yes, Suzy, I guess there is. Lots of women have fallen for Kevin before. But they all settled for what he was willing to give—a short, whirlwind affair that satisfied both parties. Kevin is always upfront. No one ever had any misconceptions."

Suzy listened carefully, her gaze resting on the top of a tall pine tree bordering a distant field.

"What I'm trying to say to you, Suzy, is that my insides tell me you're different; you're not the kind of person who could settle for that, and I think you need to know what kind of history there is here."

Suzy shook her head and her red hair gleamed in the afternoon sunlight. Whirlwind affair? What exactly did *that* mean? And how on God's green earth could anyone get that close to Kevin Ross and ever walk away?

Just then an energetic mix of Susan's dark curls and Logan's blue eyes ran up behind Susan and tackled her, saving Suzy from responding.

"Daniel!" Susan scolded laughingly, then introduced Suzy to one of her six-year-old twins. The three older Reed children were hither and yon, Susan explained, and the baby was still sleeping. And in addition, Patty Lee's four kids were here, and Logan's sister's kids, along with all their adult counterparts and sundry other friends. And, Susan added, her aunt and uncle and Logan's parents would show up sooner or later.

"Whew!" Suzy laughed as she followed her hostess up the wide porch steps. "Kevin definitely wasn't exaggerating when he called this a family affair!"

• • •

The afternoon swept by in a whirlwind of activity—races, volleyball, walks around the pond. And right in the dead center of everything for Suzy was Kevin Ross.

At one point Suzy was sitting at the edge of the dock, her chin resting on her knees, watching in amusement as Kevin baited a hook for young Daniel Reed. The kids worshiped him, she mused. Just then the line tugged and Daniel's yell rang through the air. Kevin bent over and guided the small boy's hands as he excitedly reeled in the wriggling, protesting croppie.

"We did it, Uncle Kevin!" he screeched, jumping up and down, his blue eyes flashing.

Kevin carefully unhooked the fish and dropped it into the net. Then he scooped the victorious fisherman up onto his shoulders and paraded back with fish in tow to where Suzy now stood, her face lit up in smiles.

"You guys are terrific!"

"Yeah," Daniel agreed, "we sure are!" He wrapped his arms tightly around Kevin's head and the threesome returned in glory to the crowd gathered on the shaded back veranda.

"Now *football*, Kevin!" Patty Lee's ten-year-old son, Jerry, pleaded. "Come on, everybody!"

Before Kevin had a chance to catch his breath, the kids were collecting on the wide lawn behind the house.

"This is your chance to shine, Suzy," Kevin signed across the tousled heads of the kids. "Come on!"

"You betcha." Suzy laughed and ran out onto the field, followed more slowly by several other adults.

The kids quickly appointed Kevin and Suzy opposing captains, divided up sides, and proclaimed the game begun.

"Okay, Ross," Suzy shouted, "now you'll get yours!" She hugged the ball to her chest and drew her brows together, her eyes sparkling with laughter.

Kevin turned his head to mobilize his team, but his mind's eye held the delightful image of Suzy Keller, her long tan legs planted firmly in the grass, a sprinkling of freckles shining across her nose as she bent her slender body in vicious attack. And then the game began and he watched her with unabashed delight as she ran, long legs flashing, breasts bouncing under the thin shirt, all fresh and alive and irresistible. A bevy of kids squealed and ran in protective pursuit.

The instant his hands touched her, Kevin knew he was in trouble. He tumbled her to the ground, his arms circling her waist, his hands tugging gently on the ball. He could feel her heart beating rapidly beneath her shirt, could feel her laughter tickling his cheek and neck, could most definitely feel the sensuous fullness of her breasts against his arms. He wanted to pin her there beneath him, keep this precious closeness forever.

"Oof!" With a giant shove Suzy pushed him off, flipped the ball up to Jerry's waiting arms, and leaped to her feet, her flashing smile left to soothe Kevin's defeat.

"Gotcha!" she shouted gleefully, then ran across the field.

Kevin was up and running, cheered on by flying, screaming kids. His wide smile and flashing eyes assured his team he wouldn't let them down. With one swoop he tackled Jerry, slipped the ball into Patty Lee's hands, and Kevin's team swept down the field. In a flurry of dust and grass Patty Lee relinquished the ball to Kevin as he swept by her.

Suzy saw him coming right at her, his eyes blazing in challenge, the ball clutched tightly to his body.

"I'll get you, Kevin Ross!" she whooped gleefully, then headed full steam toward his broad chest. With a swoop and a leap, she had him in her arms, captured, her feet tangling in his until they both tumbled to the grass.

It probably lasted less than a minute but seemed timeless, a delicious moment suspended above movement or thought. His body was pressed tight against hers, all muscle and heat and barely contained power. She felt his labored breath, caught the scent of him, and breathed it into her nostrils fully. It was the scent of grass and summer sun and the rich dark earth blended with the musky male odor of Kevin Ross. Like some powerful opiate it spread through her, fueling her already unbearable desire for him. The message raced along every nerve to skyrocket in her brain, and she felt herself melting, melting. . . .

"Hey, Suzy! Way t'go!" A chorus of young voices rang in her ears.

"It's all ours now!"

"Get the ball!"

Reluctantly, Suzy wheeled the football from his grasp, wrestled herself free, and flung the ball up to Logan. She felt the heat of Kevin's gaze still on her, holding her. Where his hands touched her, her flesh tingled.

Suddenly he sprang up like a lion and pulled her to her feet. Kevin knew desire for a woman well. But this was something much bigger than that. The edges weren't as smooth; the boundaries were blurred. This was something tinged and excited by the faint traces of danger. In a quick movement that Suzy barely felt, he ran a finger across her flushed cheek, then was lost in the racing array of bodies flying past.

For a second Suzy just stood there, watching the blur of color as he swept by, his broad shoulders bigger than life against the fading light of day. "Oh, Suzy," she murmured aloud, "there's something happening here that has absolutely nothing to do with pigskin." And with a shout she ran down the yard, the adrenaline surging through her body.

"More chicken salad, Suzy?" Adele Reed asked as she carefully balanced a glass bowl in her hands.

"Thank you, it's terrific!" Suzy scooped out another helping.

"Yes, it is. And Susan has graciously shared her famous recipe with all of us." Logan's mother smiled affectionately at Susan, then sat down in a patio chair next to Suzy's mother.

"It was my dowry, Suzy," Susan joked from across the shaded veranda.

Logan bent over and kissed his wife on the forehead. "Ah, my love, I must confess, I'd have married you even *without* the chicken salad."

"Oh, sure, sure." Susan tipped her head back for another kiss. "*Now* he tells me this."

Suzy watched the fond exchange and smiled. Such nice people. And so in love . . .

Her gaze automatically shifted and again searched the back lawn for Kevin. He seemed to have disappeared. Probably nabbed by some of the children, she decided as she scooped up a forkful of Susan Reed's dowry.

"Oh, my, what a small world!" she heard her mother say off to the side and listened with half an ear.

"It certainly is," Adele Reed responded. "Imagine, belonging to the same garden club, and now meeting like this!"

"And all because of the children," Bea said.

"Kevin is nearly family to us, you know. He and Susan and Logan are very close."

Bea nodded, looking down at her plate.

"And your Suzy is going to be a wonderful help to Kevin. The perfect representative for the company."

Bea dropped her voice, but Suzy still caught a snatch of her conversation. "Suzy . . . seems to be very attracted to Kevin."

Adele Reed lifted her head. Her expression was solemn, thoughtful. "Yes, and Kevin seems quite fond of her." An understanding smile softened the lines of her face. "It's interesting, isn't it, how we think we know what's best for our children even when they're no longer children. Whether it involves schools, careers, even falling in love. And how often they find someone we think most unlikely." Her gaze shifted to Susan and Logan, sitting close together on a porch swing with one of the children straddling Logan's knee. She watched them for a moment, then looked back at Bea and gently patted her hand. "Oh, you can't imagine the first time we met Susan. I thought she was telling us about the bar exam, because I could not believe my future daughter-in-law might own a bar. Bar and grill," she corrected herself, shaking her head fondly at the memory.

Bea clasped her hands more tightly in her lap and smiled thinly. "Yes, of course. But that was just a job. Something she could stop, just walk away from—"

"Oh, no! That is *who* she is. That wonderful heart and that touch of the unconventional. For William and me that was . . . well, quite a *jolt*, as Susan would say. But you know, Bea, I think perhaps their hearts often know best."

Suzy bowed her head to hide the smile that spread across her face. Adele Reed was a very perceptive lady indeed. And at least her mother was sitting and listening. One bridge crossed, she thought with relief.

When it was time for the chocolate cake to be brought out, Suzy hurried into the house to help.

"Susan," she said as she gingerly lifted the cake from its box, "Kevin seems to have disappeared off the face of the earth." She set the cake on the giant butcher block island in the middle of the sunny kitchen.

Susan retrieved a stack of paper plates from the cupboard. "Kevin? Hmmm, he's usually close by when there's food around." Her brows drew together thoughtfully as she cut the first piece of cake. "Oh, I bet I know!" She glanced at the clock on the wall. "Yes, that must be it! Come, follow me." She dropped the knife on the counter and breezed out of the room.

Suzy followed her curiously through the kitchen and up the back staircase leading to the bedrooms.

"Shhh." Susan pressed a finger to her lips and stepped lightly down the long carpeted hall, then paused before a half-opened door.

Suzy peeked over her shoulder. Silhouetted against the window was Kevin, his arms cradling a tiny form. While they watched, he walked over to the window and gently rocked the baby back and forth.

Susan smiled. "His namesake," she explained, then walked on into the room. "Kevin," she said as he looked up, "you have an uncanny sense! I didn't hear him wake up."

Kevin smiled at the two women. "Hi." He placed the baby in the crib and motioned to Suzy. "Suzy, come meet the newest Reed, my godson, Kevin Aaron Reed. Isn't he the handsomest kid you've ever seen?"

Suzy grinned at the unabashed pride in his signs. "Let me see that little wonder," she said, chortling as she stepped to Kevin's side. Tiny fisted hands reached into the air. "He knows me, Susan," Kevin signed quickly.

"I have no doubts. He'll probably sign before he speaks! And you, my friend, spoil him silly."

"A godfather's prerogative."

"How did you know he was awake?"

Kevin shrugged. Vibes were too difficult to explain in sign. Maybe in words too. It was odd, like the way he knew Suzy was near before he even saw her. In matters of the heart, there were some things you just knew. Hearing gave you no edge.

"Well," Susan said as she walked over and picked up the baby, "I'm sure you'd rather help Suzy dish up her sinfully rich chocolate cake than the other immediate option."

Kevin grinned, then nodded as Susan placed the baby on the changing table. "Tell him I'll be waiting when he's dry."

"Another godfather's prerogative?" Suzy teased.

Kevin headed for the doorway. "You bet."

"What about when you're a father? Then who changes the diapers?"

They were walking together down the spacious hallway, side by side, each suddenly aware that for the first time since arriving at the Reeds', they were alone. Suzy waited for Kevin's answer, her gaze intent on his face, but a shrug was his only reply. She knew instinctively it wasn't a subject to push. For the moment she satisfied herself with the accidental bump of his hip against hers, a gesture that seemed as intimate as a kiss.

Kevin took a tiny step away and followed it up with a deep breath. He remembered how wonderful she'd felt in the heat of the football game, that beautiful supple body firm and warm beneath his hands. He remembered . . . and took another step away.

"This has been a wonderful day, Kevin." Suzy finally broke the electric silence as they walked into the kitchen. She stared into his eyes. "Thank you for letting me come."

He nodded but didn't dare move, didn't dare close the tiny space between them. He swallowed hard. The kitchen suddenly seemed overly warm. "I'm glad you're here," he signed.

Again silence fell around them, a silence so thick Suzy felt she'd been covered with a huge woolen blanket, she and Kevin, muffled together in its folds. She waved the air in front of her face and laughed lightly. "Sure you're glad. I gave you some competition on the football field." She lifted one hand to rub his shoulder, but Kevin reached over just then for a knife. "Was I too tough on you?" she asked.

Tough on him? he repeated silently. Maybe . . . She certainly had the ability to make him feel powerless. He looked down at her smiling face and longed to trace a finger along the smattering of freckles across her nose. He set the knife down and curled his fingers into a fist, then banged his fist onto the counter. Don't touch, Ross. Not now . . . Not after that football game . . . A curious sensation almost overwhelmed Kevin, that if he did touch Suzy at that moment, if he did feel the creamy softness of her skin beneath his fingers, he would surely explode. With difficulty he took in a large lungful of air and felt it travel down his dry throat. His fingers uncurled and spoke between them. "Nah, Suzy. You're not too tough on me. I can handle it."

"Can you, Kevin?" Suzy didn't move, just stood there with her chin up, her face tipped back.

Kevin swallowed hard. "You're something else, Suzy Keller. You sure as hell cause crazy feelings inside me."

"I *love* crazy things . . ." She parted her lips, and her breathing was high and shallow with anticipation.

Thought was gone in a flash. Nothing remained but the incredible force of Suzy standing there before him, her lovely face turned up to his in honest invitation. Kevin lowered his head and brushed his lips gently across hers, a light, tantalizing touch that set them both aflame. She threw her arms around his neck, and he pulled her to him and kissed her fiercely. His mouth rubbed hungrily against hers, his tongue parting her lips and thrusting deep into her warm, sweet mouth. He cupped her face in his hands and turned his mouth this way and that against hers, pressing and lifting and sinking back into that sweetness like a man drowning—a man who did not want to be saved.

Finally he pulled away, his hands braced against the wall behind her, his eyes locked onto hers.

"Kevin," Suzy whispered, trembling. "Kevin, when is the picnic over?"

"How about right after dessert?"

"Yes!" she said, feeling her heart race to a new, unfamiliar tempo. Her tempting smile melted away any last thoughts Kevin might have had about what was right and wise and sensible.

"If it was up to me," he signed, "we'd skip right over that chocolate cake. Nothing could be as sweet as what I've got on my mind," he promised. And his kiss left no confusion as to what he meant.

Six

"Aw, Uncle Kevin, are you leaving?" the little girl asked, wrapping her arms around Kevin's leg. It was Susan's youngest daughter, Beth, Daniel's twin, and she was ready to do battle.

"Yes. Afraid so, sweetie," Kevin answered, tousling her hair. "But I'll be back another day . . . soon."

"Are you taking this nice lady with you? I like her hair! I want red hair too!"

"You are beautiful just the way you are," he assured her. "And yes, I am taking the lady with me."

"Oh! I bet you're going to play somewhere else," the little girl accused with a pout.

Kevin and Suzy exchanged startled glances and burst out laughing. "That is just what we're going to do," Kevin signed, holding Suzy tight against him. She slipped her hand into the back pocket of his jeans and rested her head on his shoulder.

"Ooooo," the little girl sang, twirling in one place and getting dizzy. "Uncle Kevin's got a girlfriend!" Covering her mouth with her hands, she ran off to spread the news.

Still smiling into each other's eyes, Suzy and Kevin pried themselves apart to say good-bye to the gathered multitude.

They met back at the van, hurrying toward it and each other with quickened breath.

Beth popped up between them. "Here. I brought you something." She held out a pinwheel, its shiny metallic fans catching the colors of the sunset. Gold. Pink. Turquoise. Emerald. "This is for you, Suzy. I want you to have it."

"Thank you, Beth," Suzy said, giving the girl a kiss on her round little cheek. "That's very nice of you."

"Yes. Mommy says I'm a very good girl."

The two adults dissolved in laughter again.

They laughed as they climbed into the van, as Kevin drove slowly down the wide drive, as he turned onto the country road and picked up speed. The sprawling, friendly house narrowed to just a speck on the horizon, then disappeared from sight. All around them were the open fields, rolling gently on in all directions, dappled green and gold with the heavy, swaying heads of sunflowers. The air was warm and sweet-smelling, redolent of flowers and ripe grains, the rich earth and the hot sun. Everything carried a feel of lush waiting, of readiness, ripeness, and fullness.

The wind blew into the open van windows and lifted Suzy's hair like a crimson banner, making it snap and fly. She caught it in her right hand and wrapped it around her fingers, leaning languorously against the door. The pinwheel, tucked into the dash, spun rainbow colors round and round. Suzy closed her eyes, concentrating on the scents and sounds carried in the window, lifting her lids for an occasional peek at the man at the wheel. When Kevin turned and looked at her, he drew a deep, unsteady breath and slowed the van.

He had to look at her; he couldn't keep his thoughts or his eyes off her. The speedometer showed 35 . . . 25 . . . 15. Suzy smiled at him. "Anything wrong?" she asked.

He shook his head and smiled back, knowing there was no way to explain what he was feeling: the dazzled, dizzying pleasure of having her so close, of having spent a perfect day with the one, the only one he'd ever love. "I'm just having a little trouble keeping my eyes on the road," he admitted.

"I know. It's wonderful, isn't it?"

"Not when I'm supposed to be driving this thing." He put both hands back on the wheel as he stepped on the gas, and the van huffed on down the narrow road. There wasn't a car in sight, just the road and the wide fields drenched in the late golden light.

Suzy ran a hand over the contour of his shoulder and down his bicep, tracing the solid curve of the muscles beneath his shirtsleeve. He smiled with pleasure at her touch and glanced at her, then away. She ran her fingers down his bare forearm, across the back of his hand, then brought her hand back to her lap. His brows furrowed in disappointment.

"Don't want to interfere with your driving," she explained, toying with the pinwheel.

He nodded, but caught the flash of her grin out of the corner of his eye. "What are you laughing at?"

"You, Mr. Ross. Do you always go to so much trouble not to get what you want?"

The speedometer dipped to ten. "I'm usually careful not to want." A wry grin pulled at the corners of his beautiful mouth. "Things seem to have gotten away from me this time."

"Lucky for me," she whispered.

Kevin looked out at the road ahead, not know-

"alluring"..."inspiring"...
"irresistible"...

Loveswept

EXAMINE 4 LOVESWEPT NOVELS FOR

15 Days FREE!

Turn page for details

America's most popular, most compelling romance novels...

Loveswept

Here, at last...love stories that really involve you! Fresh, finely crafted novels with story lines so believable you'll feel you're actually living them!

Read a Loveswept novel and you'll experience all the very real feelings of two people as they discover and build an involved relationship: laughing, crying, learning and loving. Characters you can relate to... exciting places to visit...unexpected plot twists...all in all, exciting romances that satisfy your mind and delight your heart.

And now you can be sure you'll never, ever miss a single Loveswept title by enrolling in our special reader's home delivery service. A service that will bring all four new Loveswept romances published every month into your home—and deliver them to you *before* they appear in the bookstores!

Examine 4 Loveswept Novels for

15 Days FREE!

To introduce you to this fabulous service, you'll get four brand-new Loveswept releases not yet in the bookstores. These four exciting new titles are yours to examine for 15 days without obligation to buy. Keep them if you wish for just $9.95 plus postage and handling and any applicable sales tax.

SEND NO MONEY NOW.
RETURN THIS
POSTAGE-PAID CARD TODAY!

ing what to expect next. It couldn't be, he thought. Or could it? Could she be feeling all that he was feeling, this wild desire, this perfect happiness? All of a sudden he felt like the prince in a fairy tale, just a kiss away from happily ever after.

Suzy scooted over next to him and half-turned so that her thigh was pressed along the length of his but her breasts brushed full against his arm. "I'm so glad you brought the van with this nice wide bench seat! How awful to feel the way I do and be stuck in a little bucket seat way over there."

"You'd be a lot safer."

"But, darling, we're barely moving. I could walk faster than this!"

"Your fault," he signed, shaking his head. He levered his right foot onto the gas and began to urge the van ahead, but Suzy slid a hand down the length of his thigh, from groin to knee. She let it rest there, her fingers curling over the worn, soft denim of his jeans.

The van slowed to a crawl. "Suzy." He swallowed, his eyes glinting dark and dangerous. "Suzy, this is no way to drive."

"So . . . who wants to drive?"

"Not me!" He pulled way off onto the side. Caution, be damned! With a deep breath, he pushed to the farthest corner of his mind all the fears and warnings and doubts that had filled his mind for the past two weeks. At this moment all he wanted from life was Suzy Keller. He turned and caught her face between his hands, bent his dark head to kiss her. This time, he'd worry about tomorrow tomorrow!

Suzy leaned up into his kiss, opening her mouth with bold delight, abandoning herself to his taste and feel. His breath swirled against her lips, mixing with her own, and she felt the answering swirl and rise of her passion through all her body, rippling up in waves from between her legs and spreading like a honeyed tide along every inch of her flesh.

He must have felt it, because he tore his mouth away and pressed it to the fluttering pulse at her temple, her throat, the thin, sensitive skin across her collarbone. His hands traveled down her arms and his fingers twined with hers. Silent words leaped from fingertip to fingertip. *Oh, Suzy,* he told her silently, *I want you so very much.*

He trailed his mouth across her throat, painting her skin with hot moist kisses, then lifted his head just an inch to put the fleshy pad of her earlobe within reach of his strong white teeth. He gave a quick nip, then licked his tongue around the curl of her ear.

Suzy moaned softly, the sound stealing from her lips before she could stop it. Nor could she stop the sharp catch of her breath in her throat, the liquid melting deep within her, the tingling swell of her nipples. She leaned back, giggling, and tucked her head beneath his chin, pressing her forehead against the front of his shirt. From inside his chest, booming like some great drum, she could hear his heart. So, he felt it too!

Kevin threaded his fingers through her blazing hair, circling her lovely head with his hands. He tipped her face up to his and kissed her eyelids, the tip of her nose. Reluctantly he drew his hands away. His dark eyes were smoldering with passion. "Love, oh, love . . . let me take you home with me."

She kissed his fingertips, his lips. "It's far away. An hour more."

He groaned and kissed her sweet, upturned mouth. "I'll never make it! You?"

She shook her head, grinning with delight.

"Besides . . ." He frowned, his chest heaving

with the strain of not touching her for even this second. "Besides, I wouldn't be safe on the road! I'd lose my license, not to mention my mind!"

She laughed against his mouth, kneeling on the seat and wrapping her arms tight around his neck in a sudden excess of happiness. She wanted to melt into him, to climb inside his skin and be one with him. He pulled her close, closer, hugging her tight against his chest while the steering wheel jabbed him in the ribs and the door handle poked into his spine.

"Wait." His laugh was a deep, husky rasp of pure pleasure. "Come here, darling. I've got something to show you."

He pulled her with him out of the van and around to the back double doors. With one twist of his wrist, he threw them wide. A patchwork quilt, a bit faded but fluffy and beautiful yet, lay folded in the corner.

"Oh, I see, Mr. Ross! You *always* carry a blanket in your cookie van—the better to deliver with?" she teased.

"No," he answered in soft sign, and brushed her hair back from her face as the wind tossed it about. "I put it in this morning. You can't blame a guy for dreaming."

"Dreaming what?" she asked, searching his face for the answer.

"That this is what I think it is. Love."

"It feels like love," she said, keeping his face in focus while the whole rest of the world blurred.

"Yes, it does," he answered, slipping an arm around her waist. He grabbed the blanket and led her down into the field.

They walked through the tall grasses, the sunflowers waving like parasols way over their heads. Their arms were linked around each other's waists, and their hips bumped playfully as they hurried along. Suddenly Suzy swung away on his arm, holding on to his hand and taking three or four backward dancing steps. Her eyes sparkled with flecks of reflected golden light. "Tell me, Kevin. Have you been in love often before?"

He laughed softly, surprised.

"No, really, tell me. I just . . . I just want to know *everything* about you, everything you've done and felt, everywhere you've been—" She stopped short, blushing furiously. "But you don't have to tell if you don't want—"

"Shhh . . ." He hushed her with a kiss, then answered, "I've thought I was in love before. But it was never like this." He smiled, wondering how he could have ever been so young, so silly. "It was nothing like this. After Susan took me in at the Oasis, it felt so good just to be safe, happy. To have a place, people who cared. I grew up fast, became a man fast." One dark brow dipped in amusement. "I had never thought of myself as being particularly handsome . . . sexy . . . anything like that. But . . . uh, well, there in the bar things seemed to happen."

Suzy hugged him hard, laughing in amazement. "How could you not know how handsome you are? A gorgeous hunk, that's what I'd say if anyone asked my humble opinion! So, you broke hearts, huh?"

"And had mine broken. Plenty. Once Logan had to wrestle me down to keep me from spending every cent I'd saved on a gold necklace for this little gal. But at this moment—" He paused, his hands reaching out to capture her face and hold her still for his kiss. "I can't seem to remember her name."

He bent to kiss her again, but she slipped away, weaving through the field like a bright flame among the green and gold. He chased after her and caught her, and pulled her wiggling and laughing against him. His arms circled tight around her, finding her slim and pliant as the flowers swaying in the breeze. Captured, she lifted onto tiptoe and met the sweet crush of his mouth. They kissed for an endless time while the sun slanted across the field to touch them with warmth as the clouds raced across the sky. A butterfly landed on a fly-away strand of Suzy's hair, thinking it had found a poppy or a rose among the sunflowers. When it fluttered away, it left behind a faint golden powder, like fairy dust.

Suzy felt its wings brush her cheek and gasped in surprise against the delicious warmth of Kevin's mouth. He leaned away, waving the air with one hand. "Just a butterfly," he assured her, his dark eyes laughing.

She shook her head. "*Nothing* is 'just' today. That was a magic butterfly. This—" She drew one hand in a sweeping arc. "This is a magic field. Enchanted. And what I'm feeling is not 'just' love. Not like anything I've ever felt before."

"Ah, so you have a secret past also!"

She grinned. "Very different from yours."

Reaching up, she pulled a heavy sunflower face-down near her own and shook it. The ripe seeds dropped into her open palm and she offered Kevin some. He held them in his closed hand, watching her as she nibbled and talked.

"Mine were all adolescent escapades," she said. "When I was a teenager, I used to fall in love at the drop of a hat: the lifeguard at the country club, the captain of the swimming team, a rodeo cowboy, my drama coach. It seemed all I had to do was smile and they were sending flowers, poems, love letters. . . . It was exciting, but scary. And soon there were the photographers and PR execs and ad men who told me I was beautiful, wonderful, different from anyone else they'd ever met. And after a few elegant dinners followed by not-so-elegant wrestling matches, I realized they were right. I *was* different. *Maybe* beautiful, *maybe* wonderful, but *definitely* different. I didn't want to be . . . well, in and out of a dozen beds. I decided I was going to wait, and find one man to give my heart to. He would have all of me forever. You know . . ." She smiled up at him with a kind of brave shyness. "Sleeping beauty waiting for the prince's kiss."

Kevin wrapped her in a fierce embrace and kissed her, getting a mouthful of her flying red hair for his trouble. With a laugh made rough by desire, he gathered the hair quickly in his hands, letting it cover his fingers like a cardinal's wing. And her heart beat like a little bird's against his chest, a fast flutter that caused him a swift pang of protectiveness, made sharp by passion. He wanted to hold her and keep her safe in his arms forever. He wanted to love her, possess her, surrender his strength to this magic of hers.

Letting her hair spill free, he gathered her against him, feeling that now familiar shock of excitement as their bodies molded together. His mouth covered hers, his kiss deepening as he felt her body arch and press against his in response. His hands traveled over her shoulders and back, curving hungrily around her ribs until they brushed the soft undersides of her breasts. He felt the heat of her through her thin football jersey, the straining fullness of her breasts against his chest. He leaned away ever so slightly, careful not to break their kiss, and drew his hands up to touch her breasts.

The kiss dissolved into gasps of pleasure. Suzy pulled away, reaching up to press her palms against his chest. "Wait—" She laughed, breathless and trembling. "Put down the quilt before someone sees us."

"They'd have to be in a helicopter," he signed, then shook his head in disbelief. "Look at this: My hands are shaking."

"I know what you mean. My knees are water! So put down the quilt—"

"I was looking for the perfect place. A little valley, with a bubbling stream and . . ." He took one look at her shining eyes and parted lips and tossed the quilt on the ground, bending the stalks of grass and flowers into a soft, springy nest. He dropped to his knees and reached up, his broad hands circling her waist. For a moment he knelt there, looking up at her as if she were the sun, or the first star shining in a dark sky. "Yes," she whispered. "Oh, yes!" and he pulled her down on top of him.

Laughing, she let herself fall, knowing the sure, solid wall of his chest would catch her and she could cling there, *would* cling there, come what may. Her arms wrapped around his neck and they tumbled onto the quilt, kissing, their mouths and hands suddenly hungry to explore more. They petted and caressed each other through their clothes, rolling playfully across the quilt, first one, then the other on top.

Suddenly Kevin broke away. His eyes were glazed with a dark, burning desire. "Slowly. Slowly, love," he told her, his sign melting into a touch so exciting it made her breath hiss through her teeth. He drew his fingers across her lips, down the pale column of her throat, and over her breasts. Slowly, lightly, he played his fingers over the thin jersey, around the full outer curve of her breasts, making quivers of excitement race across the tender flesh. And even as she trembled, his fingers plucked at her taut, straining nipples, rolling them between his thumb and forefinger.

"Oh," she gasped, arching up against his hand. "Oh, Kevin. I want you. . . ."

Pain darkened the flash of exultation that blazed across his face. "I'd give my life to hear you say that!" he signed, and his arms quickly circled her as she leaned up against him, giving him a hug that knocked the breath right out of his lungs.

Her huge eyes were damp but blazing when she pulled away. With surprising strength she pushed him back onto the quilt and leaned over him, her hair falling across his cheek. "Oh, I know, I understand. But I hold your life too dear for you to give it up just to hear me talk. There are other ways to say what we want to tell each other. Here, watch . . ."

She unbuttoned his shirt and tugged it free of his jeans, then spread it open to expose his chest. His bare, bronzed skin glistened with a sheen of sweat. She pushed her fingers through his dark curly hair, then traced the words *my darling Kevin* across his skin. Their eyes met. Ducking her head, she brushed her cheek against his chest, loving the feel of his hair, the wide bands of muscle, the beauty of him.

"Just what are you doing?" he signed, his eyes smoky with arousal.

She drew her lips and tongue slowly and sensually across his skin and felt him suck in air in a huge gasp of pleasure.

With a shaky laugh she answered with a question of her own, her eyes wide with wonder. "Don't you think it's amazing? Right this moment we're new to each other. Unknown. Strange and wonderful. And in moments it will all be different. Not just known and shared, but . . . but sort of belonging to each other, you know?"

"Yes," he answered. "Yes, I know exactly what you mean."

He framed her face with his hands, smiling deep into her eyes. Curving toward her, he kissed her with an incredible sweetness, a soft, lingering kiss full of promise. Suzy felt the earth spin, and tumbled into his waiting arms.

He lifted her on top of him and wrapped his legs around her, pinning her to him at the knee, thigh, groin. She felt the heat of him, the unmistakable power of his arousal, and she began to melt and throb, the waves of desire rising to lap along her burning flesh.

"Wait . . . wait!" she said. "I wanted to show you . . ." But he kissed her words away, biting them from her lips, licking them from her tongue.

His hands circled her ribs and he lifted her up against him until his mouth found the engorged tips of her breasts. His teeth nipped at her through her top and she moaned and writhed against him, stirring him to an agony of arousal as surely as coals stirred to flame.

Burning, he rolled her over onto the quilt and leaped up. "Another minute and I'll explode!" he signed, his face taut with tension. "Damn, look what you're doing to me, darling!" Laughing deep in his throat, he tore his clothes off and tossed them aside.

He knelt beside her and with slow, heated sensuality drew the edge of her jersey up over her ribs, her breasts, right up and over her head. She heard his reaction, the rough catch of his breath and its sharp release as his dark gaze lovingly caressed her: the tanned skin across her breastbone, dotted with summer's freckles; the paler, smooth-as-satin fullness of her breasts; their dusky pink and hardened tips.

Barely moving, she lifted her hips and slipped

out of her shorts and panties, his hands helping to tug them down over her calves and feet. Trembling, quivering with anticipation, she stroked his shoulders, the muscled span of his back, the hard curve of his buttocks.

"Oh, Suzy, I love the way you touch me," he told her, bending his head to kiss her breasts. He took first one nipple then the other into his mouth, licking her, tasting her unimaginable sweetness. He used his teeth gently, but her body answered with a fierce rush of desire and demand.

"Now . . ." she cried. "Oh, love me, Kevin, love me now . . ."

"Soon," he whispered, his hand falling from the sign to touch the honey-gold fleece between her legs. He covered it with his palm, his touch circling slowly, with mounting pressure, feeling her body flame with the same passion that had him breathless and burning. He stroked the silken inside of her thighs, urging her on. *Come to me, come to me,* his touch instructed.

"Kevin!" With a soft cry of abandon, she curved up against him, burying her face against his chest, rubbing the pleasure tears into his hot, flushed skin. She bit him, nipped at him, licked her tongue across his throat, then found his mouth and pressed her lips to his, sobbing with desire. "Kevin, I want you to love me—"

"Suzy . . ." It was a whisper, a fragment of a prayer breathed against her lips. With a desperation almost painful he gathered her beneath him and covered her with the burning length of his body. Parting her thighs, he slipped between them and she felt the wild fierce thrust of connection as they became one.

"Oh, oh!" She breathed in little gasps, laughing, crying, as their bodies learned the other's secret rhythm and delights. With great love and restraint he carried her higher, higher, bringing her pleasure she had never even dreamed of.

"Love, oh, love," she moaned.

His heart heard her. Lifting his head, his eyes gave her a glimpse into his soul. *I love you*, he said silently. Then she felt the world explode and spin, flashing its rainbow colors, a wild spinning pinwheel of happiness. And with a low growl of delight, Kevin unleashed himself and surged on with her into ecstasy.

As soon as he could move again, Kevin rolled beneath Suzy, placing his body between her and the quilt. It was full dusk now. The sun had dipped beneath the horizon and only a last golden light spread hazily across the sky. The sunflowers tossed and nodded far above them, and the crickets were tuning up for their nightly symphony.

Kevin smiled. The weight of her lying limp and spent in his arms made his smile widen. Her breath was an even whisper against his chest, and she barely stirred when he reached across her and drew the quilt up over the two of them. Lazily, filled with great content, he drew gentle patterns across her bare skin. Her name. His. And other words: love, beauty, joy. A deep sigh lifted his chest, his breath sifting her hair over his shoulder but leaving her undisturbed. Yes, there were other ways to say what needed to be said.

She pushed herself up to look at him. "Oh, Kevin, I'm so happy here. I think I want to stay here forever." She snuggled down against him, rubbing her toes against his ankles.

"It's getting dark," he signed halfheartedly, not really wanting to leave either.

"If we close our eyes, we'll never know." She laughed and rubbed her breasts against his chest.

He laughed too. "If I close my eyes, this conversation is over!"

"Oh, I forgot!" She giggled madly and had to kiss him once just because she had to. Then she frowned, puzzling over something that tickled just at the edge of memory. "I know!" she exclaimed, poking him gently in the chest with one tapered finger. "You said my name aloud, didn't you? Now, don't try to deny it! I may have been floating on another planet, but I heard you. You said 'Suzy,' didn't you?"

"Blame it on the heat of the moment," he signed. "Lost my head or something." He grinned. "Which is easy to understand, when you remember the moment."

"I remember it perfectly," she assured him. "But don't you try to change the subject. If you *did* say it, then you *can* say it. Will you again, please?"

He shook his dark head slowly, his gaze never wavering from hers. "No. I'd rather not."

"But why not?"

"Because this . . ." He tightened his jaw. "This suits me fine."

"It suits me fine too. I just thought the other would be nice. Sometimes. On *special occasions. . .*" She winked at him, shattering the brief moment of tension with her bright smile. "You know, someone famous once said: All the great pleasures in life are silent. Nice, huh? Though I don't think I was very silent . . . and neither, my darling man, were you!"

She reached for her clothes. He could see her shoulders shaking, her breasts quivering, the smooth skin across her belly jumping with laughter. Being teased by this laughing, naked woman, this wood nymph, this sprite, was the greatest happiness he had ever felt. Laughing with her, he put on his clothes and gathered the quilt in one arm. The other he wrapped tightly around her waist, holding her close to his side as they walked out of the field.

"You know," Suzy said, looking back over her shoulder as they reached the van. "I'll always have a special fondness for sunflowers."

They drove home in the dark. She was nestled against him, half dozing, wrapped in contentment. When the lights of the city filled the car, Kevin slowed. They were nearly home.

Suzy looked out the window, watching the passing lights. Home, she thought. But the city wasn't the same as when she'd left it hours before. No, that wasn't quite right. *She* wasn't the same. And would never be the same again. This day with Kevin had changed her. She'd wanted it, asked for it, but what she'd received was almost overwhelming, bigger than life. She shivered slightly and pressed closer to Kevin. She'd never given of herself like this before, so completely, so lovingly. What now, Suzy? she asked herself. Had you thought of that? What have you and Kevin done to each other? Where do you go from here?

When he stopped for a red light, Kevin shifted and looked down into her shadowed face. "Shall I take you home, Suzy? It's late. Or maybe my place?"

It's late . . . My place? His small but cozy apartment attached to the back of the warehouse? Suzy's mind was fogged. She couldn't seem to get her thoughts straight. Her lips moved slowly and her hands shook beneath Kevin's intense look.

He felt the hesitancy in her body. "It's okay, Suzy, I understand." He captured one of her hands in his and held it steady, then brought it slowly to his lips before releasing it. "It's a lot to process all at once like this. You need some time alone."

Her gaze drifted out the window again. She did need time alone—time to separate dream from real life, to step out of her feelings and look at them in the clear light of day. But she couldn't, not yet. If it *were* a dream, she wasn't ready to wake up. Not quite yet. She shook her head against his shoulder and brought her gaze back to his face. "Could we . . . could we stay together just a little longer, Kevin?"

I'd brave fire and flood if you but asked, my love, he thought. But he only smiled and signed, "Sure, Suzy . . . a little longer."

Seven

The mattress tipped slightly in Kevin's direction and Suzy rolled toward him, eyes closed, arms opened wide. She circled his bare, lean waist and rubbed her hands across his fuzzy chest. "Ummm . . ." she purred, tightening her grip and snuggling closer, but he unwound her arms and swung his legs over the edge of the bed.

One sleepy emerald eye popped open. Then the other. No. This was no dream. Kevin was the most real man she'd ever met! The thought made her grin like a Cheshire cat, all pleased and satisfied, and happiness bubbled in her throat and escaped as a husky laugh. "Come *back* here," she chided before tackling him again from behind.

He fell back onto the bed, laughing, his dark eyes full of love and mischief. "Just what do you think you're doing?" he teased, hurrying through the signs so that he could bury his hands in the fiery spill of her hair. He gathered handfuls and held it back from her face as he kissed her ripe, sweet mouth.

She kissed him back and settled happily right on top of him, her long legs sandwiched neatly between his, her weight resting on the wonderful strength of his body. A little ship riding on the powerful sea, that's what she was, she thought. A little ship . . . and this felt so wonderfully right that she must have found her port . . .

"I'm trying to keep you here in bed with me," she said in answer to his question. She nipped his bottom lip, catching it between her teeth and giving a sharp little love bite.

"Ow!" He yelped aloud, then laughed and growled and rolled over on top of her, holding her tight. His face was flushed with arousal. He pinned her between his knees, then sat up, grinning. "You are full of spice today," he signed. "A surprise. I thought you'd wake up all shy and sleepy after that wild night. . . ."

"It's just that . . . Well, I'm so happy, Kevin!"

A blazing smile lit his face, but as if he were afraid to let it show, he pulled on a serious look. "Well, I thought I would get dressed and put on the coffee—"

"I don't want coffee. And I *don't* want you to get out of this bed."

"And what exactly *do* you want, dear one?"

Reaching up, she wrapped her arms around his neck and hung there like a jewel against his chest. "I want you. I want the taste of your mouth and the feel of your hands on my skin and everything wonderful that follows. I want to see fireworks again with my eyes closed. Oh," she added blandly, all mock-seriousness, "by the way, how do you sign 'fireworks'? Show me."

He brought his hands up between them and signed, "I've got something else to show you first!" He laughed and nuzzled his chin into the hollow of her neck. His beard roughed her tender skin and she wiggled beneath him, trapped there between his knees. Yet suddenly he was the one trapped by his own uncontrollable passion, by the fire burning out of control in his loins and across every inch of his flesh. He dropped his weight full upon her, dusting hot kisses across her face and breasts and belly. And there they were again, making love when he should be making coffee, his brain said, but nobody was listening.

Later they lay face-to-face on their sides, studying each other with solemn eyes.

"I must be dreaming," Kevin told her, his fingers brushing her nipples as he signed. "You are the most beautiful woman in the world, Suzy Keller. Beautiful and funny and wonderful. I *must* be dreaming."

"Yes, I've wondered about it too. But if it's a dream, Kevin, then let's never stop." She lay still, rolling the dark hairs on his chest between her thumb and index finger. The skin beneath was tan and smooth as suede and suddenly terribly erotic. All night that had been happening to her. She'd notice one single, otherwise innocent part of his body and become fixated by it: his mouth, the hollow of his throat, the hard curve of his biceps, the smooth power of his thighs. Now she tugged at the hairs on his chest, grinned, and walked her fingers slowly down his body, past his belly button, and into an even thicker patch of hair.

"Oh, no, you don't!" he warned, catching her wrists in his hands, then dropping them and signing roughly, "Stop! You are making me crazy, woman."

"That's what you get for unleashing—hmmm, I wonder how you sign *that*?—anyway, for unleashing all this wildness in me. Now I'm going to make you pay!"

"Dear one, the only thing I'm going to pay for right now is *dinner.* Get up!"

"Dinner?" she echoed. "What time is it?"

"Late afternoon . . . of the day after."

"Ohhh." She yawned, then nestled down into the warm covers. "It was the nicest day I've ever spent. But I don't think I slept a wink, and now I'm very . . ." She yawned again, hiding her mouth behind her hand. "Very sleepy."

He smiled and brushed the tangled hair off her cheek. Then he escaped from bed, tugged on his pajama bottoms, tossed the tops back to her, and headed for the kitchen. There was a whir and soon the smell of fresh ground coffee wafted back into the bedroom, but Suzy didn't notice. Snuggled into his striped pajama tops, she was sound asleep on his pillow.

Kevin paused in the doorway, holding a steaming mug in each hand and the afternoon paper tucked under one arm. At the sight of her his knees buckled and he leaned heavily against the doorframe. This *had* to be a dream, a dream that would fade and leave him lonely. He had sworn never to want, never to let himself be vulnerable. He had thought he was immune. Damn, how wrong could a guy be?

"I love you," he whispered in a voice made rough by long disuse. This may be crazy, impossible, he thought, but he did love her. It was as clear to him at this moment as the lovely smile on her face. And he was going to enjoy that love for now, no matter what the future brought.

He strode over to the bed and set the mugs on the night table, then leaned over and brushed his lips across hers. Suzy stirred, looped one arm languidly around his neck, and smiled. "I think I drifted off again."

"Time to get up, sleepyhead. There's not a thing to eat in the house and I'm starving."

He yanked the covers off the bed, picked her up, and carried her into the shower.

Suzy fussed and wriggled. "Oh, no! Don't you dare, Kevin. I'm not ready to wake up. Oh, you wouldn't! Help!"

The water was hot and wonderful and, as the bathroom windows steamed, they played in it like two children, scrubbing each other's backs and piling mounds of soap bubbles on noses and shoulders. Kevin washed her hair and it spilled over his hand like claret wine. She sudsed the dark springy hair on his chest, then stood on her toes and pressed her breasts against him, sending soapsud islands floating down his lean, hard torso. Eyes clenched shut, he held her tight in his arms, feeling the pale satin of her skin burn through his flesh and into his heart. The water stung his face and rolled down his cheeks, but he didn't feel it. All he knew was that this was impossible, but it was all he wanted.

"I'm turning into a prune!" Suzy said. She laughed breathlessly and pulled back against the circle of his arms. She swung her hair in a shining arc, sending water flying in all directions. "And now, Mr. Ross, *I'm* starving. You're either going to have to love me or feed me. . . ."

A fierce desire flamed in his dark eyes, but he let go of her, turned off the water, and grabbed two thick terry towels from the rack. Then, barefoot and dripping, he padded into the bedroom and returned with the no longer steaming mugs. They sipped the coffee, stealing glances over the rims. Suzy dried her hair while Kevin shaved, and when he was done, she lifted onto tiptoe again and rubbed her cheek against his.

He kissed her with incredible yearning, then tore his mouth away. "Go get dressed," he signed, pushing her toward the bedroom.

"Oh, you're making this difficult."

"My darling Suzy, we need air." He tickled her stomach with his signs, "And food. One of us has to see to the basics!" His hands moved up and circled her breasts before he gently spun her around and headed her toward her clothes.

Since Suzy's jersey and shorts weren't suitable attire for dining out, they drove to her apartment, where she changed into an attractive short-sleeved blouse and a full cotton skirt. Then they drove back to the warehouse and left the van to walk to a restaurant Kevin often went to.

Hand in hand and in dreamy happiness they strolled through the dark sultry night. Faint light shone from an occasional warehouse window and spilled from the white globes of streetlights. The trees were motionless; there wasn't a hint of a breeze. Half a mile to the north a tugboat pushed a barge up the Mighty Mo, sending its hollow wail echoing over the warehouse district.

Suzy stopped to listen and Kevin raised one questioning brow.

"Tugboat," she answered. "I used to think it sounded so sad, but not anymore. Not ever again."

"Dreamer," he signed, shaking his head. "You're a hopeless romantic."

"And you?"

"I thought I was a realist. All the way. Knowing what's possible, and what's impossible." He looked down at her as he added, "But now I'm not so sure."

She pressed his hands to her chest and kissed him fully on the mouth. "Yes, I know. But let's not analyze it tonight. Instead, let's get something fantastically huge and delicious to eat and be fantastically happy. All right with you?"

The little restaurant was just over the Twelfth Street Bridge, and they ate barbecued ribs and cole slaw and fries until they thought they'd burst. There was a combo playing jazz, rocking the tiny place with bass and drums and a wailing sax. Suzy caught Kevin drumming time on the table-top with the flat of his hand, so she made him dance with her. He argued at first, glowering at her, but she saw the laughter in his dark eyes and knew she was safe and pulled him onto the floor. He danced with an easy athletic grace, hold-ing her close and swinging her away in a loose, sexy lindy. All the men were gazing at her, approv-ing, admiring, desiring, but Suzy saw only Kevin.

When the set ended, she sank back into her chair, fanned her neck with her napkin, and daz-zled him with a smile. "How do you *do* that? Tell me, do you hear it?"

"A little, just the heavy beat of it, the way I can hear the slam of a racquetball. But mostly I feel it, from the dance floor right up through my body. Again, like the rhythm on the courts. Or when Logan and I sail. I don't have to hear him call the swing of the sail, I can feel it through the move-ment of the boat on the water, anticipate it almost."

"It's wonderful. It's like magic."

"It's practice, that's all, darling. Besides, you have to remember, my experiences at Susan's Oa-sis Bar. In the mornings, or after closing, when it was just us—the 'crew'—Jerome would play his sax, and Susan would dance around the bar with Logan or me or the mop, whatever was at hand. We were a pretty relaxed group."

"It sounds wonderful! So wonderful, I'm jeal-ous. That's what you did while I was dragging from agency to agency, sitting absolutely perfectly still for hours under hot lights with everyone fuss-ing at my hair, my makeup, the way I tilted my head. Taking acting lessons and ballet lessons. Studying every minute in between so I wouldn't flunk French or algebra. Going to parties where I wanted to talk about books or movies or the newest dance and everyone else just wanted to talk about my body or my face. . . ." She stopped short, catching little shallow breaths between her parted lips.

"Suzy . . ." Kevin was shaken by a sudden fierce protectiveness, the need to hold and love her and keep her safe. The depth of his feeling shone in his eyes, and Suzy felt it and blushed.

"Sorry," she whispered, her perfect lips tipped in a crooked smile. "You know, that's not at all like me. Actually . . ." She dropped her chin into her hand, her elbow resting on the table. "I've never said any of that to anyone before. But I've never felt like this before. It's as if I've just awakened from some long sleep, like Sleeping Beauty, locked in the castle for a hundred years, waiting for her prince. Well, all my life I've been the center of things, caught up completely in my career and my mother's plans and dreams, and they've been like a wall around me, keeping me safe, but keeping the world out. It's like I've never *seen* the world before. And *you've* woken me up. Now I know what I've missed, and . . ." She stood up, grabbing his hand. "And I want to go out and walk around, look at the river, the stars, the stars shining on the river. . . ."

"The stars shining in your eyes."

"And yours! Oh, you are so wonderful, so brave and strong."

"Come on, let's get out of here!"

It was after midnight, but they walked back across the bridge and down to the river's edge, holding hands and smiling at each other through the darkness.

Kevin vaulted onto a narrow stone wall and drew Suzy up beside him. They watched the black river, the water seemingly still and solid in the dark, except for where it foamed and bubbled as it swept around the pillars of the highway bridge. Cars zipped by overhead, their lights piercing the night more brightly than any star. Overhead the constellations hung pinned to the velvety sky. A small dark shape whirred by, then others, skimming the river just in front of them like black pieces of paper flung by some unseen hand.

Suzy gasped. "What was that? Birds?"

"Bats, probably," Kevin answered.

She shivered and snuggled closer against his side. "Maybe we should go back to the apartment now. It *is* getting late. . . ."

Grinning, he jumped to the pavement. He put his hands around her waist and lifted her down slowly, letting her slide lightly down the front of his body. She leaned there, her weight balanced against him, her arms wrapped around his neck. "Now I know we should go home!" she teased, and they laughed softly.

They were just two blocks from the warehouse when Kevin felt Suzy tense suddenly. She hesitated midstep, looking up at him with eyes wide, and began to turn. Instinctively he spun and jumped in front of her, shielding her with his body, but it was too late.

Three men leaped out of an alley and attacked them, grabbing Suzy and pulling her away, hitting at Kevin with fists and baseball bats. He felt the searing pain of a blow on his upper arm, then across his shoulder, and he fought to get away from them, to get to Suzy. The man holding her had shoved her up against the wall and was trying to rip her pocketbook off her shoulder.

"Take it!" she cried. "Take it and go away. Don't

hurt us!" But the punk grabbed her arm and went for her watch, her rings.

Kevin swung wildly, shaking off one attacker and backhanding him into the wall. He turned on the other and slammed his fist into the man's face, feeling the hot spurt of blood on his hand.

Then the crash of a bat on his back drove him to his knees, blinded, his head ringing. Nausea and oblivion reached up to claim him. He couldn't pass out now! Suzy! He looked up through a red haze and saw the mugger push her roughly to the ground. "Suzy!" Shouting her name harshly, he scrambled to his feet and threw himself on the man's back, slipped an arm around his throat, and jerked him over backward. He landed with a thud and lay motionless. Kevin wheeled around and grappled the nearest punk, jerking his feet out from under him. He jumped on top of the man and knocked him out with a sure swift uppercut to the jaw, then crouched to meet the rush of the other. But the mugger, bleeding from Kevin's first blow, turned to flee.

Kevin exploded after him, a black arrow aimed at the man's heart. He tackled him to the ground, grabbed the front of his shirt, and would have scrambled his face, but someone grabbed his uplifted arm. Shaking with fury, he yanked his arm away and aimed the blow again, but the same two slender hands fastened on his forearm. He looked up. "No," Suzy cried. "No, Kevin. Enough! The police are here! Kevin, please—"

He froze, cold sweat pouring from his body, the adrenaline still burning in his veins. He glared down at the punk on the pavement, his eyes filled with murder. He wanted to kill these creeps for scaring her, for hurting her. *Was* she hurt?

His fierce gaze caressed her face, softening as it lingered on the disheveled hair clinging to her pale cheeks, her wide panicked eyes and trembling chin. "Okay?" he asked.

She nodded, big tears filling her eyes. "But are *you*?"

Before he could reassure her, a heavy hand fell on his shoulder and he turned to the uniformed policeman. "It's all right," the officer said. "We'll take over now." Another policeman yanked the mugger away.

Kevin pulled himself to his feet and grabbed Suzy, hugging her tightly against him. Then he released her. "Darling, little darling," he signed, "are you hurt? Oh, God, did they hurt you?"

"I'm fine, Kevin, just fine. But you . . . You're bleeding and your mouth is all swollen and—"

"Folks," the officer interrupted. "Are you all right? Anyone need an ambulance?"

They both looked at Kevin, but he shook his head.

"Then I'm going to need a statement here. Tell me exactly what happened." He took out a pad and looked at Kevin, but Suzy spoke. "We were just . . . just walking along and these three . . ." Her voice wobbled and tears rolled down her cheeks again.

Kevin tightened his hold, pressing his bruised cheek against her hair.

"Why don't *you* tell me, sir. It might be easier."

Kevin's white-edged lips tightened grimly and his eyes narrowed with a dark bitterness.

Unaware, Suzy nestled against him. "He's deaf. But, officer, there's not much to tell. They jumped us, started beating Kevin with those bats, and one tried to—"

"Stop!" Kevin signed in fury. Dammit, he couldn't even get her home safely. Couldn't keep her from getting hurt. Self-loathing cut like a knife in his gut. Another minute and he'd explode all over the damn street! "Give me the paper," he signed, and grabbed it from the officer's hand.

He scrawled the facts, shoulders hunched against the twisting pain in his heart.

Oblivious to his thoughts, Suzy saw only the blood on his cheek, his set jaw, his fierce independence. Oh, he was magnificent. "Magnificent . . . but crazy!" she muttered, reliving the fear she had felt as he battled the three muggers. He could have gotten himself killed!

She rubbed a hand over his back, felt his quivering, unyielding fury, and mistook it for exhaustion.

He shrugged out from under her touch and thrust the pad back at the policeman. "Tell him I'll come to the station if he needs more information. I wrote down Mike's number. Tell him to call."

"Kevin, he could call *me* and we could go down together."

"Tell him to call Mike!" He almost spit the signs.

Suzy flinched. "Fine, if that's what you want." She was glad he couldn't hear the hurt and dismay in her voice.

Spinning on her heel, she faced the officer and his partner, who had just handcuffed the three muggers and was leading them to the patrol car. She answered the remaining questions and assured both officers she was fine.

"You're sure?" one asked. "How about a ride home?"

"Take it!" Kevin interrupted.

"You think we should . . ." she began tentatively, but he stopped her words with his fierce signs.

"*You* take it. At least *then* you'll be safe. Go!"

"She bit back the angry retort that leaped to her lips and stared up at him, measuring him with

her emerald gaze. Suddenly she understood. Oh, Lord, what a proud, stubborn man
he was! But she could be just as stubborn!

"Thanks," she said to the policemen, "but we're
almost there. We'll walk." She tucked her hand
in Kevin's arm.

The officers exchanged a skeptical glance. Suzy
smiled and added clearly so Kevin was sure to
see, "Don't worry, Mr. Ross will take care of me."

With a quick salute they were gone.

"Well." She tipped her head back and met
Kevin's glowering stare. "It's just you and me,
kid!"

"You should have gone with them."

"I didn't want to."

"When we get to my place, I am taking you
right home. Where you are safe. Where you
belong!"

"Pardon?" Suzy said, all wide-eyed serious-
ness. "I didn't understand what you said."

Growling, he caught her hand and marched
off. Suzy had to run a few steps to keep up with
him, but then she lengthened her stride, her
long legs a good match for his, and easily kept
pace. They took the warehouse steps two at a
time. "I'm just getting the car keys," he signed,
"and I'm taking you home."

"Not till I wash off that cut on your cheek, and
put some ice on your lip."

"I'll take care of that later. You're going home
now."

"Pardon? I didn't understand."

"Cut that out. You understand everything!"

"You're right, Kevin, I do. I even understand
that it's not me you're angry at. And not even
those muggers. You're mad at yourself."

He spun away, effectively ending the discus-
sion. But Suzy was tougher than he thought.

She slipped ahead of him, plastered herself against his front door, and folded her arms firmly across her breasts. "I'm not leaving until we talk."

"I'm not talking!"

"Fine. Then I'm not moving." She fixed her gaze on the middle of his heaving chest and stared, calm as a clam. After a full minute of silence she added, "I have a whole lot more practice at holding a pose than you do, Mr. Ross. You may want to send out for breakfast."

Again that husky growl of pure frustration. Kevin stepped closer, put one finger under her chin, and tipped up her face. He stared deep into her eyes, then heaved a sigh. "You mean it, don't you?" he asked.

"You bet." She smiled wryly. "People often think that because I look the way I do, that I'm all fragile and soft and easy to get around. I wouldn't want you to make that mistake."

He brushed the back of his hand across his aching cheek. Everything hurt, inside and out, and if he didn't sit down soon, he'd fall down. "Fine. But you can only stay a minute. Then you'll call a cab and—"

"Pardon? I didn't understand."

Gritting his teeth in exasperation, he pulled her into the apartment.

Inside, he cupped one hand under her chin and pushed the damp tendrils of her hair back with the other. His handsome face was gray with exhaustion and worry. "Are you really okay?"

"Yes. Just very scared."

"They didn't hurt you? No cuts, no bruises?"

"No, Kevin."

"Sure? I saw him push you down."

"But you were too fast, too strong! He never had time to hurt me. All I got was a scraped knee."

"Let's see." He dropped heavily to one knee and lifted her skirt. A little dried blood was caked on the roughened skin. He looked up, his face gone from gray to white. "Does it hurt?"

"Oh, silly! You wonderful, silly man. I had worse skinned knees when I was a kid riding my bike, or roller-skating. Once I even fell out of a tree!"

"Don't tell me—" He closed his eyes in pain.

"Silly man!" she murmured, blinking back tears that threatened to fall on the top of his head. She wove her fingers through his thick dark hair, and he wrapped his arms around her thighs and leaned his head against her.

She ruffled his hair, shaking loose bits of twigs and gravel. Fresh blood was oozing from a thin cut on his temple and on his cheek.

She took hold of his shoulders and pushed him slightly away. "Your turn for a little tender loving care. Come sit down."

With difficulty he rose to his feet, then staggered to the nearest chair. He sprawled in it, his head falling back, his long legs stretched out in front of him. Suzy ran to the kitchen and got a bowl of warm water, some clean towels, some ice. Gently she pushed the hair back from his eyes and dabbed at the cuts on his face. He flinched, grimacing in pain, and started to pull away. "I'm okay!" he signed.

"Sure, Superman. Well, just let me play Lois Lane for a while, or I'm calling your friend Logan and telling him to meet us at the hospital."

"Don't. You'll scare Susan and the kids. Really, I'm okay." He forced a grin. "I'll behave."

"About time!" She leaned down and brushed a kiss gently across his lips, then apologized when he yelped in pain. "Here." She wrapped ice in a towel and handed it to him. "Now, sit still."

She bathed his face, then unbuttoned his shirt and helped him slip out of it. The bruises on his shoulders, back, and arm were already turning an ugly purple. She tried to be gentle, but she could see the sheen of sweat rise on his body, the pain flash in his dark eyes. Scared, she asked again, "Are you sure you don't want me to call a doctor?"

"No. I'm just sore. Tomorrow I'll probably feel like I got kicked by a mule, but nothing's broken. Really. Stop looking so worried."

"Easier said than done, mister."

"Come here." He pulled her down on his lap. His hands traveled over her in the gentlest of caresses. "Now, I want you to call a cab, and I want you to go home. Better, I want you to go to your parents' house. And I want you to sleep late and stop thinking about this. I can't stand to see that look in your eyes."

"Then let me lie down in your bed. I promise to close my eyes and we can hold each other tight, and then neither of us has to be worried."

"No."

"Why not?" she whispered.

"Because the sooner you leave, the better. Suzy, I am damn serious. This is not going to work."

"*Why not?*" she repeated, getting angry now.

"Are you crazy? I almost got you killed tonight. I never even heard them coming!" He pushed her off his lap and stormed across the living room. "Don't you understand that? Another man would have *heard* them."

"Maybe. But *I* heard them only a second before they jumped us. What matters is that you saved me, Kevin."

"And I almost killed those three men." He looked down at his hands, his face a mask of pain and bitterness. "And you know what, I would have too. Without blinking! And that scares the hell out of me. Suzy, when I was a kid living on the streets, I was tough. I had to be. There was no one to love, no one to trust. I held my own life cheap. I had to fight and hate . . . and I knew how. But, Suzy, *your* life I would cherish. It would make me crazy. I'd always be seeing dangers out there, something that could hurt you that maybe I wouldn't be able to save you from. It would make me crazy, Suzy!"

"Kevin, I don't *want* a guardian angel." She smiled wryly. "Don't you think my parents have done enough of that? What I want is a lover and a friend."

The longing in his eyes was a flame he quickly quenched. "Find someone else. It can't be me."

"Too late!" She marched right up to him, eyes blazing. "You already qualify on all counts. Or did last night not mean anything to you?"

His hands shook as he signed, "You *know* what it meant to me. More than anything. More than my life."

It was true. Her heart knew it was true. Now all she had to do was make him stop being so darned stubborn! But how? She pressed her fingertips to her aching temples.

"Are you all right?" he asked.

If Kevin had been looking anywhere but into her emerald eyes, he might have seen a little light flash on over her head. Those years of acting lessons were not for naught. "I—I suddenly feel very weak," she murmured, fluttering her lashes. "Ohhh . . . I do feel faint—"

He caught her in his arms and lifted her close against his chest. A groan of pain escaped his lips, and for a moment Suzy felt horribly guilty. She knew how sore he was, how tired, but desperate times called for desperate measures. She let her head roll gently against his shoulder, forcing her breathing to become shallow. So gently, he placed her on the bed and sat down beside her. She felt the heat of his thigh against her hip, the coolness of his palm against her cheek. But his hand was shaking.

Biting her lip, Suzy opened one eye and peeked up at him. "Hi there."

The pain etched across his face made her repent immediately. "Oh, Kevin . . . dear one, I'm fine." She scrunched her face into a mournful frown. "I'm sorry. I didn't mean to scare you. I just wanted to get us back in each other's arms, back here in this bed, on friendly ground."

The pallor of fear was banished by a dark flush of exasperation. "Suzy Keller!" he signed, relief making his hands fly. "You are impossible. I don't know what to do with you!"

She laughed, throwing her arms around his neck. "Love me."

His flush darkened and she could see the erratic beating of his heart in the hollow of his throat. He looked at her for a moment, then turned his face away. The lamplight streaming in the bedroom window lit his profile and dusted his shoulders in gold. Her own giddiness softened to something much more tender and sultry.

She fell back against the pillow, but kept her hands on his body, drawing her palms across the solid planes of his chest, around his rib cage, down over the small of his back, and beneath the waistband of his slacks. His whole body tensed with a fierce urgency.

She clasped him in her arms and pulled him down against her. As his hard chest crushed her breasts, she whispered in his ear, "I love you, Kevin Ross."

Did he hear her somehow, or did he merely feel the stir of her breath against his ear? Either way, he pushed himself up and looked at her strangely, his whole body trembling.

"Stop!" he signed. "Suzy, you don't know what you're saying. You're young, excited, full of life. You don't know—"

"I know I love you."

"No, you don't. You know *I* love *you*. And that *is* true. But you don't know anything about the other. You only think you do because you've always gotten everything you've wanted. Your life's been so golden."

"Well, maybe the world is harder and scarier than I thought, but with you I suddenly feel very brave and adventurous."

"Suzy, don't—"

"Why not? Oh, I'm making you blush, but I don't care. I think you're wonderful, and it's not because of your deafness. I forget about that. No, it's the thought of sharing my days with you, my nights, my dreams . . ." She ran the tip of her tongue over her dry lips. "I mean, I know we're not up to that yet, but somehow I feel we—" Hot tears stung her eyes, but she blinked them back and held her chin up. "We're connected, you and I, heart to heart."

"You don't know what it would be like—"

"Then *tell* me."

"I can't."

"Then let me tell you. We'll have a lovely whirlwind courtship while your cookie business skyrockets and my career soars, and then we'll have a lovely, but very private wedding, and we will be fantastically happy for a while, and then we will have some beautiful babies and be even more fantastically happy—"

"And their father will be deaf!"

"Yes, he will be." She nodded solemnly.

"And"—his dark eyes burned into hers—"during this whirlwind romance, when we meet your friends, you'll have to interpret for me, reading my signs—"

"Yes, I will—"

"And at parties, when the conversation flows like wine—"

"*Yours* will sort of limp along, until I get better at interpreting."

"And you think your friends, the kind of people you associate with, will have patience for that?"

"Kevin, I don't associate with dummies! They'll know a great thing when they see it, a man of remarkable courage and talent. And the fact that *I* cannot sign perfectly will not turn them off."

He gritted his teeth and rolled onto his back, hands clenched behind his head. His broad chest rose and fell rapidly, and the lamplight made the curly hairs look like a warm, soft pelt. Suzy gave in to a wanton urge and tangled her fingers in his hair.

"Stop that!" He fought back a grin and brushed her hand away. "And what about your *career*? You think those big-time agencies are going to like the idea of a deaf boyfriend? Cocktail parties and shootings and interviews . . . I'd only be a problem, dammit!"

"Wrong! Oh, that just goes to prove how wrong you are! If it was any of their business, and if we'd let them, which we won't, they'd probably milk it for all it's worth. They'd make you stand glowering and gorgeous in the back of all my photos. And they'd probably want the wedding to take place on *Phil Donahue*, the wedding pictures on the cover of *People*! Oh, you'd only be an asset, Mr. Ross. But, to tell the truth, it's really none of their business. What I model and for whom I model has to do only with how well I can sell their product. It has nothing to do with the fact that the man I love is deaf."

"Suzy, Suzy . . . don't say that." His face twisted with longing. "Please, don't make me believe it." He kissed her face, her ears, her hair.

"But I want you to believe it. You *have* to believe it."

"Suzy, you don't know what you're saying."

"Then watch what I'm *doing*." Eyes flashing, she knelt next to him on the bed and began to remove her clothes, skirt . . . blouse . . . slip. . . .

His indrawn breath hissed through clenched teeth. "I should be stronger," he signed, and his breath escaped in a groan.

Suzy smiled, dimpling. "You're the strongest man in the world. The bravest, the handsomest—"

He reached out and touched her breasts, cupping her warm pale flesh in his palms, then rolling the pink nipples between his fingers.

The pleasure of it arced down through her body and she was melting, aching. Suddenly it was no game, and the seductress became the seduced. When he leaned up, rubbing his cheek back and forth across her breasts, back and forth, she wanted to cry or scream. Wanted him to touch her, hold her, fill her again. And then he caught one nipple between his teeth and tugged. Her bones were water and she tumbled onto him, and he touched her down low, and the magic of loving swept over them again.

Eight

"Was 'the picnic' really only two weeks ago, Kevin?" Suzy asked as she tugged her suitcase out of the back of the van. "The picnic" had become a special code, a symbol of the happiness that circled around the two of them like a soft cloud.

"Two weeks, one day, and two and a half hours," Kevin joked as he locked the vehicle, then guided Suzy into the airport. He felt her laughter as they entered the terminal. It was wonderful. Everything about Suzy Keller was wonderful these days.

"This'll be a great trip, Kevin. I've always wanted to neck on an airplane."

He wrinkled his brow in mock reprimand.

"Actually, Kevin, it might be our last chance. We should take advantage of it. After the *Today Show* broadcast, everyone will know who we are—"

"*You* are, Suzy."

"Whatever. Our private life will have to be kept *private*!" She threw her arms around him in the middle of the terminal, her lovely green eyes locking onto his. "But if I attack you now, no one will even blink."

He brushed a kiss across her smooth cheek, then wrapped an arm around her and guided her toward the gate. Who was she kidding? he thought. Every male within seventy yards was watching Suzy Keller with wide-eyed, unabashed lust. Instinctively he pulled her closer.

He wondered later how he'd lasted those endless miles between Kansas City and New York with Suzy pressed so closely to his side—and not even the hope of a cold shower. He'd tried to submerge his libidinous hunger by eating everything in sight: his dinner, *and* Suzy's, *and* the poor lady's across the aisle who wanted only to nap. And two Scotch and waters helped down the fires burning in his veins.

Nevertheless, the hotel was a welcome sight. When they'd gotten settled and Suzy pushed gently on his door from her adjoining room, he opened the door so quickly she nearly fell through into his arms.

"Kevin? Were you leaving"—her gaze traveled the length of him—"in your robe? I should warn you, it's turned quite chilly out."

He grinned. "No, dear one. I was about to invite you in for a nightcap. To calm the nerves before the big day."

She swept into the room, her own robe tied tightly around her waist, her face glowing. "Oh, Kevin, I can't believe it's happening!" She sank down onto a soft upholstered couch near the marble fireplace and curled her legs up beneath her. "Me, Suzy Keller, on the *Today Show*! Who would have thought . . . ?"

"Anyone who has known you for longer than ten seconds." He poured them each a glass of brandy from the well-stocked bar and sat down next to her. "I have to admit you were right from the start," he teased her, stroking the soft burnished waves of hair curling over the edge of her robe.

"What do you mean?"

He let her hair slide from between his fingers and signed, "Hiring you. I'm not often talked into things. But this time I'm very glad I was."

She looked up at him, then set the brandy down on the glass-topped coffee table. "Yes," she said, and the sound came from deep in her throat. "Yes, I'm glad too. I told you what it was, remember?" She wrapped one arm around his neck and drew herself close.

"Kismet." He pressed his lips hungrily to hers. Yes, he remembered. His fingers slid down and loosened the sash of her robe, then slipped quickly beneath. Smooth naked flesh welcomed his touch and Kevin moaned into her sweet-smelling hair. Had fate brought him Suzy Keller? Kind fate! His hands traveled eagerly over the silken smoothness of her inner thighs and lingered at the soft, fleecy nest between her legs.

Suzy's sigh stirred the hair behind his ear and she reached into the folds of his thick robe, her fingers sliding across his chest. "Oh, Kevin," she breathed. She bared his chest as her lips kissed the skin her fingers warmed, then brushed across his nipples and teased them to firmness.

His own hands never stopped their tantalizing movements, gently, eagerly, stroking her until her head was spinning and her lips pleaded with him urgently to come to her.

Their robes fell away as Kevin slipped over her, covering her quickly with his body. The chilly autumn gusts outside the window were as far away as the earth itself as they spun heavenward in each other's arms, exploring worlds neither had ever known before. Yes, Kevin thought in a blinding flash of light, it must be kismet.

•   •   •

"Just go on over there." A young woman holding a large clipboard nodded at Suzy, smiled at Kevin, and pointed beyond a large camera to what seemed like the only uncluttered spot on the whole set.

Suzy smoothed her emerald silk dress down over her hips and glanced up at Kevin.

He looked at her lovingly and nodded, then signed an answer to the question in her eyes. "Yes, Suzy, you look just lovely. Perfect, in fact." He brushed a kiss as light as a butterfly's wings across her forehead, then pulled back and gazed into her eyes. "Now, just stay calm and do your thing."

"Oh, Kevin. Please come on with me."

"Suzy." He drew out the sign as his look speared into her like an arrow. "I *never* appear on television. That's why I hired *you*!"

She grinned nervously. "Okay, okay. But what if my throat goes dry and I can't talk?"

"Take a drink of water."

"I might spill it! Right there in front of all of America, Suzy Keller spills a glass of water down the front of her dress. Ohhh, Kevin," she moaned, nervously biting her lips. "And what if I can't think of anything to say?"

"Suzy, if there's one thing you've never had a problem with, it's that." His signs swept the air firmly.

She poked him gently in the ribs. "Oh, shush. Well then, what if—" She sought her scattered thoughts for another random fear, but Kevin stopped her words with a finger placed carefully over her lips, before signing, "Then I'll fire you!"

"Oh." She flashed him a bright smile. "Then I'll just have to do a perfect job!" She threw her shoulders back and took a deep breath of air.

"Ms. Keller? Up here, please." The same efficient

woman motioned her up to the familiar-looking set.

Suzy's gaze darted back to Kevin's face.

He smiled encouragingly, kissed her soundly, and nudged her forward. "Don't worry, I'll be here the whole time. You'll be great!"

She smiled faintly, then turned and followed the woman over to a comfortable chair.

"This is where you'll sit, Ms. Keller. Is there anything I can get you? We'll be on the air in a few minutes."

Suzy shook her head and swallowed hard. "No, thank you. I'm just fine."

The woman checked with a cameraman, then disappeared, and Suzy sat down.

Lights switched on and she blinked, then slowly adjusted her vision and looked around her. Heavens, how silly to be nervous, she thought. These furnishings were almost as familiar as her own. How many times had she seen these very chairs on her TV set? With everyone from Bruce Springsteen to Margaret Thatcher sitting on them. Ohhh! She wondered briefly if she was going to be sick. No! She couldn't do that to Kevin. She'd be just fine. She'd been on television dozens of times, after all. And who cared if the viewing audience was five million—five million?—the cameras looked the same, right? She smiled up at a cameraman. Sure, she'd be fine. For Kevin.

"Hello, you must be Suzy Keller."

A tall, friendly blond woman walked over to her and held out her hand.

Suzy fell into a familiar smile and sighed out loud. "Hello, Miss Pauley! How nice to meet you."

"Please, call me Jane." The lovely hostess sat down beside Suzy. "And how nice to meet *you*! I've been reading my notes on Kevin's Kookies and can't quite believe what a wonderful success story we've found here."

Her friendly, enticing chatter went on and Suzy warmed to it, falling into the conversation so easily she hardly noticed when the cue came and the show began to air.

She was talking about Kevin, after all. It was *his* story she was telling to America, and that was a story she didn't need cue cards or prompters for. *That* story was written on her heart.

"Yes, Jane, Kevin is quite wonderful," she said. Her throaty laugh drew the cameraman close. "He's a real twentieth-century Superman!"

"Is it true we'll soon be seeing even more of Kevin's Kookies here in New York?"

"Absolutely. We have a special spring promotional campaign lined up for your city. Colorful carts filled to the brim with Kevin's Kookies will dot the streets of Manhattan. We're even introducing a special flavor for New Yorkers. But it's a secret. You'll have to wait and see." Her teasing smile filled the camera's lens.

Jane Pauley chuckled at Suzy's contagious enthusiasm. "But the largest secret of all is Kevin Ross. This bigger than life entrepreneur who has beaten the odds life dealt him and risen to such incredible heights . . ."

"Yes. And he shouldn't be kept a secret. He's . . . he is wonderful!" Suzy's heart swelled with love and pride. She looked off into the dark shadows where Kevin was watching. "He's right here, Jane." Her hands swept through the air as she pointed toward a stunned figure who stood glued to the cable-ridden floor.

He must have read her lips wrong, Kevin thought. She couldn't be saying what he thought he saw! He took a step backward and glanced at a nearby monitor. Suzy was still looking in his direction!

"He's here?" Jane Pauley graciously beckoned him forward. "What a wonderful surprise for our early morning audience. Not only do they get to meet the lovely Suzy Keller, who will soon be seen in a massive advertising campaign for Kevin's Kookies, but they get to meet the man behind the whole story, Kevin Ross."

Kevin's stomach lurched and his heart beat erratically. Damn! he thought. What was she doing to him? But there was little choice left as the cameras turned slowly and waited. They were waiting for *him*. Millions of Americans who hadn't even eaten breakfast yet were waiting for him! Kevin commanded his feet to move, his heart to beat normally, and with a forced nonchalance he walked over to the two smiling women and held out his hand to the *Today Show* hostess, Jane Pauley.

"Kevin Ross," she greeted him, "welcome to the *Today Show*."

Kevin smiled grimly and sat down in the chair next to Suzy, who was looking at him with those damnable wide, wonderful eyes. He leaned back in the chair, silently swore some favorite, rather colorful curses, and decided to make the best of it.

"Kevin began with nothing," Suzy started in, and Kevin looked out toward the cameramen to see if they had the good sense to focus on her and not him.

"And the very first idea for this venture, how did that come?" Jane asked.

Suzy paused for a moment and looked at Kevin.

"The Waldo Street Oasis crew, remember?" he signed to Suzy as the camera recorded every gesture.

"Oh, yes!" Suzy said, and enthusiastically went on to tell the whole story. Kevin found himself falling into the mood and shifted his chair so he could see both women's lips, interrupting whenever Suzy needed help.

Before long, Jane Pauley was no longer interviewing a deaf person, but a successful, intriguing entrepreneur. The three in front of the camera communicated like old friends. Kevin and Suzy were a team, and together they were giving Jane Pauley a story she'd remember for a long time. She could read Kevin's handsome, expressive face, and, as Suzy expounded later, her hero had impressed the socks off everyone, from the hostess to the cameramen to the millions glued to their TV sets.

Finally, Jane reluctantly began to bring the interview to a close. "It has been a real treat having you both with us this morning, Suzy Keller and Kevin Ross," she said. "Two very special people with exciting careers ahead of you. Kevin, we wish you the very best with your business, and we'll certainly look forward to your spring campaign." She smiled engagingly. "I *do* hope the New York special has at least a hint of chocolate!"

Kevin's easy smile gave nothing away.

The hostess turned to Suzy. "And you, Suzy Keller, are certainly off to a wonderful start in your modeling career. I have one last question for you, Suzy, before our time is up."

Suzy nodded and smiled in anticipation. She was almost hating to see the interview end!

"With all the exposure Kevin's campaign will give you, Suzy, we know you'll be propelled right up that ladder of success. What I'd like to know, Suzy, is when this initial campaign is over and you've sorted through the many offers that are bound to come your way, what will be next? Where will we next hear and see Suzy Keller?"

Suzy's face went blank. Next?

Jane Pauley continued. "Will it be high fashion? Movies? What do *you* see in your future?"

Kevin's hands clenched into fists and his heart thudded to a stop. Reality exploded in his head like a bomb. *What's next, Suzy Keller?* Movies? High fashion? That meant Hollywood. New York. Paris. A continent away. A *world* away. Damn! Suzy had spun such a spell around him, he'd blocked it all out. Reality. The future. The rest of the whole damn world.

Notice, he told himself grimly, Jane Pauley had not made the mistake of saying *their* future. Not their future, but *her* future! Anyone could see there was no future for the two of them together. Oh, he was a success, admirable, inspiring, worthy even of several minutes on national TV . . . but he *was* deaf. All these people knew it; they hadn't forgotten for one second. Only *he* had forgotten! A mistake you'll pay for, Kevin Ross, he swore. But you'll pay for it alone.

Narrowing his eyes against the pain, he watched the face he had come to cherish as Suzy innocently, naïvely, thought through her response.

"Well, Jane," Suzy said, her voice faintly bewildered, "we've been so busy with this campaign that I haven't had time to think about it! I mean, we've all been so completely involved in making the campaign a success that thoughts of the future haven't even been relevant. I think I'd like to pass on that question for now, if you don't mind, and we'll just see what tomorrow brings. . . ."

Kevin hardly noticed the closing remarks or felt the congratulatory pats on his back as he guided Suzy out of the studio. He felt numb and in agony at the same time. He'd been careless. Worse, he'd been a damn fool. And now he—not kismet or fate or luck—would have to set it straight.

Nine

"I'm sorry, Suzy, but that's all I know," Ethel said. "He's in L.A., staying at the Beverly Wilshire. You two are becoming quite the jet-setters!" She laughed, then continued more seriously. "But, Suzy, you were *with* Kevin. I can't understand why he didn't fill you in on the details himself."

Suzy clutched the hotel phone. "Well, Ethel, I guess he didn't want to bother me. I slept late today and . . ."

"I can understand that, Suzy. All the excitement of the show and all. You were absolutely fantastic, by the way. And so was Kevin. The phone hasn't stopped ringing since nine A.M. yesterday!"

Suzy let a small smile curve her lips. "Well, that's good, anyway."

"Are you coming home today, dear, or staying on in New York for a while?"

Suzy paused for just a moment. "Ah, no, Ethel, I won't be coming home just yet. There're a few things I need to take care of first. . . ."

"Excuse me! Pardon me! Out of my way, please,"

135

Suzy exclaimed as she made a mad dash through the Los Angeles airport later that day.

LAX was seething with vacationers, commuters, kids selling roses, tour guides gathering their camera-laden flocks, and Suzy felt as though she had spent far too much time in airports lately.

The highways leading into the heart of Los Angeles were no better: crowded, stifling, the pavement shimmering with the white heat of midday.

The cab slowed to a stop in front of the grand old hotel on Wilshire Boulevard and a uniformed doorman ushered Suzy into the cool, silent lobby. She drew a deep breath, resting one hand on the back of a velvet chair. Oh, the luxury of polished marble floors and jeweled chandeliers, lush plants gleaming in a crystal atrium, the decorous approach of the bellman with her bag. She had shlepped that thing from New York, through Kansas City International and Dallas International, and she never wanted to see it again!

"Madam, will you be checking in?" the bellman asked politely.

"Certainly. I am joining someone." There, that sounded plausible, right? Now, if it only worked that way.

When she reached the registration desk, the clerk looked up and smiled. "Yes, may I help you?"

"Yes. Kevin Ross's room, please. I am joining Mr. Ross." Her smile made the desk clerk wish she were joining *him*. Not to mention that body, that face. Now, where had he seen that face before? Was she an actress . . . a movie star?

"Excuse me," Suzy prompted. She fluttered her eyelashes, knowing full well the effect that would have on the already enchanted young man, but all was fair in love and war. "Sir? Mr. Ross's room number, please."

"Oh, oh, yes. Certainly." He typed in the appropriate code and quickly scanned the computer monitor. "Here we are. Now . . ." He hesitated, horribly afraid of offending this vision. "I have to call up to the room. House rules."

"Of course. But . . ." Suzy let a faint frown crease her brow. "Mr. Ross is deaf."

"Oh, Mr. Ross, Right! I was supposed to remember that. He even gave me a note for the guest he's expecting. . . ." The clerk turned and fumbled in the mailbox numbered 1515. "Right! I thought he had said for lunch, but I guess I misunderstood. So sorry, Miss—"

"That's quite all right." She held her hand out for the folded note.

"S. E. Kanasawa?" the clerk read off the white paper, his face mirroring total confusion.

"Thank you." She offered a smile in lieu of an explanation and turned toward the bank of elevator doors. "Fifteen-fifteen did you say? And . . ." Her emerald gaze dipped to his nametag, then swept back to his already flushed face. "Thank you so much, Robert." Love and war, right, Keller? She tucked the note, still folded, into her pocket.

The elevator whisked her and her luggage to the fifteenth floor in less time than it would have taken her to come up with an appropriate greeting, let alone an excuse for having followed him to L.A. Fifteen-fifteen was at the far end of the hall and she hurried toward it. She didn't *want* time to think.

A modest knock brought no response, so with an apologetic grin tossed at the bellboy, she slapped the door hard with the flat of her hand, then bent and wiggled the note underneath the door.

Kevin pulled the door open, tugging the knot of his tie into place with his free hand, his business smile already in place for Steve Kanasawa. He froze.

She heard his breath catch in his throat and saw the smile vanish from his lips. Anger, frustration, desire, and despair all warred in his dark eyes. Anger won.

"What are you doing here?"

Oh, boy, Suzy thought. Maybe this was a mistake. If she hadn't been just too exhausted to move, she would have turned and fled. Instead, she lifted one shoulder in a little shrug, whispered, "Hi," and slipped under his arm and into his room.

Kevin stood like a statue, muscles tensed and quivering along his arms and shoulders. When he turned and glared at the bellhop, the poor fellow took a quick step back. "Sir, I . . . uh, the lady's. . . ?"

Kevin jerked a thumb back toward the elevator.

"No, don't listen to him!" Suzy waved the boy in, her panic subsiding now that she was comfortably collapsed on the sofa. "Please, bring my bag in. Don't let him scare you. His bark's worse than his bite."

"I wouldn't bet on it!" Kevin's signs were fraught with danger, and the fellow dropped the bag in the hall and left fast.

"Kevin, be sensible. I'm already here."

"Be *sensible*! Me? You show up on my doorstep, three thousand miles from where you're supposed to be, and tell *me* to be sensible. The last time I saw you, you said you were exhausted. You wanted to sleep all day, quote, unquote!"

"With you!" she retorted, but he ignored her interruption.

"Suzy, you are supposed to be in New York, resting, relaxing, having the time of your life."

"Sorry, Kevin." She sighed. "I didn't understand what you said."

"Are you going to start that again?" He strode closer, scowling down at her. "Look where it got us last time."

"I am perfectly happy with where it got us, Mr. Ross. It got us all snuggled up in bed, you and me and our assorted toes and noses and shoulders and legs and . . ." She grinned, a crooked little grin full of mischief. "And that's where I'd like to be right now!"

Kevin stalked across the room and sank wearily onto the foot of the bed. How in heaven's name was he going to handle this woman? Her . . . and the feelings she woke in his heart?

The red message light on the phone began to blink. What now? he wondered. He dropped his head into his hands, then glared up at her. "That must be my banker. I have got to take care of business, Suzy."

"Go right ahead, dear. I won't be in the way, I promise."

"You're right. Because you're going to stay right up here until I get back."

"I may. Or I may go to Disneyland. Or tour Universal Studios—"

"Suzy!"

"I only said I may. I may also just take a long hot silky bubble bath and lay right across your bed and watch the soaps. Nothing dangerous!"

Ha! He swore silently. Just the thought of it made him dizzy with desire.

Suzy got up and strode across the room to sit beside him. She smiled up at him. Rubbed her cheek against his shoulder.

"Cut that out! Suzy, this is a mistake."

"I know. You should have gotten a king-size bed."

• • •

Just a quick half hour later, feeling refreshed and rather risque, Suzy strolled through the lobby to El Padrino, the restaurant in the hotel. The restaurant was decorated in a Spanish motif, with rust-colored tiles on the floor and black wrought iron everywhere. It was split into different levels, and tables were arranged for privacy . . . or, better yet, Suzy thought, cozy intimacy. Still, she spotted Kevin immediately. He and another man were sitting at a table near the door, a margarita in front of each of them.

Kevin was trying to keep his mind on business. He was trying damn hard not to think about Suzy in the tub, or sprawled across his bed. But somehow he missed Steve Kanasawa's last remark.

"Pardon?" he signed.

"I was just saying, now is the time to explore the California market. And my family would like to discuss a franchise arrangement in Japan." He waved aside Kevin's skeptical frown. "It sounds like a real possibility to me, Kevin. The figures these last two months in Chicago and Washington, D.C., were phenomenal! The gross in Chicago alone outdistanced your projected sales by—"

"Not too fast." Kevin signed carefully, then wrote the rest of his thoughts on a yellow pad in his bold, slanting scrawl. "All that sounds great, but I don't want to go too fast. I'm interested in a future for this company, for myself and all my employees, not just some fly-by-night, pocket-the-proceeds operation."

"I understand that. And respect that. I just wanted you to know of the interest you're generating out here."

"Great. Now, I'll need you to draw up a sample contract that we could use here, and—"

Suzy stepped through the doorway. She was

dressed in a slim black suit edged in silver thread, her blazing hair knotted under a daring little hat and veil. She looked utterly mysterious and desirable.

When she smiled, every man sitting near the door stared. Kevin sat stock-still, his hands clenched beneath the table, his knuckles white.

Steve Kanasawa flicked a quick grin his way. "*My* fantasy would be that she'd just walk over to this table, smile, and say, 'Hi. Mind if I join you?' "

Suzy touched her fingers lightly to the pearls at her throat, drew a deep breath, and strolled over. "Hi. Mind if I join you?"

Steve choked on his martini. Kevin gave him a good solid swat on the back, rose, and pulled out a chair for Suzy.

"So," she said, smiling, "how's business?"

"Suzy Keller, Steve Kanasawa." Kevin scribbled the names on his pad.

"Suzy Keller? The Kevin's Kookie girl?" The young banker stared at her with unabashed pleasure. "Honest, I didn't recognize you. In the ads, you look so young, so girl-next-door."

"That's what Kevin wanted. And what Kevin wants, Kevin gets."

"Like hell!" Kevin signed.

"Good thing you didn't say that aloud, sir," Suzy replied, her green eyes twinkling. "They'd throw you right out of this fancy restaurant."

The air above their little table began to hum with electricity.

He wanted her, Kevin admitted to himself. And didn't *want* to want her! He wanted to be left alone with his nice, difficult business problems.

"Oh, no," she said as though she had read his mind. "I'm not leaving you two to business. You've spent too much time like that already, Kevin."

Switching to sign, she added, "That's what makes you such a crab!"

He wanted to throttle her. Hug her. Kiss her. Throw her on the floor and make love to her. The tension was like a taut silken cord connecting them to each other.

Suddenly they both realized that Steve Kanasawa was looking from one to the other like a spectator at a tennis match.

"Sorry," they apologized quickly.

"Hey, that's okay! Go ahead and argue if you'd like. I know how great that feels, to be able to say what you're really thinking in front of strangers and not have to worry. I myself enjoy it on occasion. As a matter of fact, there's a terrific Japanese colloquialism that I favor. It would translate to something like 'Oh, go jump in a lake!' but sounds a lot more ferocious. Just about Kevin's style."

"See, look at the reputation you're getting!" Suzy teased.

"Just since I met you," Kevin answered. "Before that I was a real sweet guy."

She reached across the table and touched his cheek. "You're still a real sweet guy. The sweetest guy in the whole world. That's why I followed you all the way out here, despite plane changes, delays, tired feet, et cetera, et cetera, et cetera."

Steve again looked from one to the other, then coughed into his fist. "Uh, would you two please excuse me? I'll be back in a moment."

And without waiting for an answer, he flashed a smile and exited quickly.

Kevin glared at Suzy. "You shouldn't have come."

"But why? Why did you walk out on me? 'I'm going to get a paper,' you said, and that's the last I saw of you. No good-bye, no I love you. . . ." Tears gathered unbidden, clinging to her lashes.

Kevin took her hand and pressed it to his lips.

Oh, Lord, the last thing he had wanted was to cause her any pain. "I never meant to hurt you. I was trying to keep you from getting hurt. It was the only way I knew to put some distance between us. Suzy, this relationship is not possible for us. For *you.*"

"Why?"

"Because I am a street kid who did okay. And you're a princess. Sleeping Beauty, you said so yourself. Well, it's time you woke up."

"Hey, you can't use my own story against me! That's not fair."

"Nobody said life was fair," Kevin answered, and raked his fingers through his crisp, dark hair.

"Well, *I* intend to even out the odds a bit!"

Steve returned and Kevin held back his retort. But Suzy's comment stuck like a burr on the edge of his consciousness.

When lunch arrived, Steve and Suzy munched contentedly on their filets of sole while Kevin chased his steak around his plate with murderous intent.

After he had whisked their plates away the waiter asked, "Would anyone care for coffee? A brandy?"

"No, thank you," Steve said quickly, reaching for his attaché case.

Kevin also declined, eager to get the check and be gone.

"Yes, Courvoisier, thank you." Suzy smiled graciously at the waiter and rested her chin on the palm of her hand.

Both men sank back in their chairs.

"Suzy . . ." Kevin narrowed his eyes. "Don't push your luck."

"Luck?" she retorted. "I don't ever want to hear that word again. Luck? Ha! Chance? Fate? *Kismet?* Double ha! I thought I was the luckiest girl in the world. I mean, I went for a job interview and met the man of my dreams. But . . ." She drew a deep, melodramatic sigh that caused her lovely breasts to press against the pale, thin fabric of her blouse, and at least half a dozen assorted men broke out in cold sweats. "But . . . ah, from now on I believe only in hard work. Perseverance. Stubbornness. I've got the fight-for-what-you-want-attitude now, and I've got it good!"

"Go try out for the Chicago Bears, then. It's not going to do you any good here."

"We'll see." She smiled and turned her face slightly away, letting her gold-tipped lashes rest against the cream of her cheeks. But then, she told herself, all was fair in love and war, right, Keller?

Suzy sipped her brandy with maddening languor.

Desperate to fill in the silence, Steve Kanasawa told them about his family's banking interests in Tokyo, his years at Berkeley, and his young wife, just newly arrived from Japan.

"Oh, my goodness!" Suzy said. "What an adjustment. Marriage and a new country all at once! I do hope she's happy in her new home."

"She is. Oh, sometimes she gets a little lonely. You know, it takes a while to make good friends, and I'm tied up with business a lot of the time."

"Well, while I'm here, maybe we could get together. We could go shopping, or . . . even better! We could be real tourists and go to Disneyland, or—"

"You are *not* going to be here that long," Kevin interrupted.

"Great!" Steve said. "I'm sure she'd love the company."

The two men's answers collided in midair, and Suzy chose not to see Kevin's signs.

"Wonderful," she said to Steve. "Here, give me

your number and I'll call her in the morning to make plans. Okay?"

Caught between Suzy's irresistible charm and Kevin's undeniable ire, Steve quickly made his farewells. "See you tomorrow, Kevin. I'll bring those contracts and we can iron out the rough spots." Then he fled.

"What a nice man," Suzy said. "I like him."

"And he obviously liked you," Kevin signed. He crushed his napkin and tossed it onto the table. "Can we go now?"

"Up to *your* room?" she asked a little loudly, somewhat breathlessly, her eyes shining with mischief.

All the men around them held their breaths.

Holding his own, Kevin slipped one broad hand firmly under her elbow and propelled her from the restaurant. "You are a vixen!" he signed, glaring at her as the elevator rose toward the fifteenth floor.

"Desperate times require desperate measures," she quipped.

Kevin unlocked his door and let her slip by into the room. He stopped in the doorway, his heart thudding against his ribs. The whole room was filled with the delicious scent of her bubble bath, that subtle, slightly citrusy scent that spoke of her pale breasts and silken thighs. And his sheets were rumpled, the blanket tossed back, his pillow holding the imprint of her head. It made him crazy, wild and crazy with yearning.

Dammit! How was he supposed to be strong when she tormented him like this? He was only flesh and blood, after all. And he *wanted* her, wanted to hold her, touch her, kiss her.

"Kevin, let's not fight," she said, wrapping her arms around his waist. "Come inside and talk to me. Whatever it is that's got you so worried, we can work it out. I know it!"

He held her, the silken threads of her hair snagging against his dry lips. She was everything he had ever dreamed of, everything he had forbidden himself to dream of because he was *deaf*.

"You are wrong, Suzy, unless you know some magic formula that can make me hear again. Some potion? Some spell? *I* have tried everything else: the specialists, the hospitals. They have *no* solutions. So who are you—"

"I'm the woman you love! The woman who loves you!"

"But why? Why do you love me?"

His innocence and the deep hurt it revealed tore at her soul. Tears slid down her cheeks. "Are you crazy? You happen to be the sexiest, the smartest, the bravest, the most endearing, the most attractive—"

"Sorry I asked!" he interrupted roughly, his eyes oddly bright. He turned away, but she slipped in front of him again. "I love you because you are you. And that's everything I want."

"There are other men who will make you happy. Once I'm out of the picture, you'll find them."

"And what about you?" she challenged him.

"I will be fine. I have my work. I have my friends."

"Is that enough?"

"It will have to be."

"But why? Why settle for friends, as wonderful as they are? Why not someone who will love you above all else? Why not someone, one single someone, who will share all your dreams and hopes and triumphs . . . and even your troubles? Why not me?"

"Because I can't let you."

"Because you are so impossibly stubborn! Or are you punishing me because I didn't have a quick answer in front of millions of strangers on TV?"

He flinched as if he'd been slapped. "Oh, God, Suzy, you know that isn't true. I just want you to face the truth. You need to fall in love with a man who can match your dreams: glamour, success, fame—"

"Well, thanks so much for defining my dreams for me, Kevin Ross!"

"Suzy, you're just making this harder. That's why I left New York, so you could spend time alone with those people, the people who will shape your career . . . your future. They loved you on TV. There's no telling where your career could go, and they know it. They would tell you to be sensible, realistic, just like your parents tried to warn you from the start!" He gave a mirthless little laugh.

"Kevin, don't tell me you're still worried about what my parents said, how they acted? That's forever ago! My falling in love wasn't a part of their game plan, no matter whether the man be president or football player or you. Give them a chance. They've changed, Kevin. They respect me enough to believe how I feel about you."

He shrugged helplessly, suddenly at a loss for words.

"Here, I'll *prove* how wrong you are." She reached for the phone and dialed Kansas City. With the first hint of a smile since they entered the room, she held the receiver out to him. "Here. I'll go pick up the extension. Imagine, a phone in the bathroom. I'll feel positively decadent!"

Kevin cocked his fists on his lean hips, one dark brow arrowing into his hair.

"No?" she said. "Well, that shows you how desperately you need my help. You've lost your sense of humor, Mr. Ross—

"Oh, Nikki, hi! It's Suzy. Listen . . . What? Oh, I'm glad you loved the show. Mom and Dad too? Great!" She had carefully turned to face Kevin so that he could read her lips. "You're kidding? Dad taped it and sent it to Grandma O'Brien? Fantastic! Oh, no, they didn't! Their bridge club? And he wants Kevin to speak to his Rotary Club? Now there's a compliment from Dad! Now, listen, Nikki, would you please get—

"Yes, yes, I know, Nikki, he *did* look great, didn't he? I know, he *is* so impressive, and . . . What? Yes, very charismatic, I agree." She winked at Kevin's unyielding scowl. "Your prom? Well, I don't know, sis. I'll have to ask him. . . . No, I don't suppose he *has* ever been asked to chaperon a prom before. I know *I* haven't! Now, Nikki, would you please—"

Suzy dissolved in giggles and slapped one hand over the mouthpiece. "Nikki says if you won't marry me, would she do?"

Kevin shook his head. She was crazy. Her sister was crazy! How did one argue with crazy people?

"No, Nikki, I'm not in New York. I'm in Los Angeles. . . . No, silly, not alone. Kevin's here too—

"Stop that gasping, Nikki, and listen. Yes, I'm sure you'd love to be here too. . . . Now, would you please . . . Nikki, shut up!" she said laughingly. "There, that's better. Now, as much as I love chatting with you, I called to talk to Mom and Dad. Would you please get them?

"They're not there? *Now* you tell me, Nikki!" Suzy's groan filled the room as she said good-bye and hung up the receiver. She looked over at Kevin and focused on the trace of amusement lighting his eyes.

"Well, Kevin, you get the idea, don't you?" She lifted one shoulder questioningly as her gaze searched his face. When she spoke, her voice was low and husky, but Kevin read her lips perfectly. "I think they like you well enough."

Kevin didn't know whether to scoop her up in his arms or throw himself out the nearest window. This woman . . . and now her family, were making him crazy. Was he the only sensible person in the whole mess?

But Suzy didn't wait for an answer. She rushed over to him and hugged him, lifting onto tiptoe to press her flushed cheek to his damp, slightly raspy cheek. Damp? She pulled away but he was quicker, turning his back and heading for the bar.

He poured himself a hefty shot of Scotch and downed it in one gulp. The burning in his throat was a good excuse for the burning behind his lids, he thought. Besides, what further words could he offer against that shining naïveté of hers? He'd have to bide his time and do what needed to be done later. But not *too* much later or he might just start to believe that magic of hers.

Suzy took his silence for surrender. And, pleased with her first victory, she decided to mount a major offensive.

"I think I could do with a little nap before dinner. Want to join me?" Without waiting for an answer, she slid quickly out of her clothes until she stood, all silken limbs and lush, ripe curves, in a tiny lace-trimmed teddy the color of pale amber.

She heard the hiss of his indrawn breath and felt the familiar excitement begin to fizz through her body. Lifting her hair off her shoulders, she stepped closer, and closer still, till her breasts pressed against the hard, smooth wall of his shirt-front. She kissed his throat, feeling the erratic beat of his pulse beneath her lips, and the underside of his jaw, and the full, sensual curve of his lower lip.

He pulled her tight against him, smothering her with hot, fierce kisses, his tongue twining around hers with a gentle yet urgent suction that seemed to tug at all the secret places within her. She clung to him, weak-kneed and yielding, feeling her breasts swell and ache, their pink tips pressing taut against the silk of her teddy. And she felt his response, his muscles hardening against her softness, the rising thrust of his arousal hot against her belly.

With a groan he pulled his mouth away and buried his face in her hair. Dear Lord, the words he wanted to whisper to her! The things he would give his life to say: that he loved her; that she was his world, his sun, and his moon; that every word she spoke, his heart answered.

Twisting away from her, he signed instead, "I am going to take a shower. You . . . stay here!"

Too startled to reply, she stood and wrapped her arms around herself, cold and shivery after the heat of their kiss. She heard the sharp ping of the water against tile, and frowned. So, the war wasn't over yet? she mused. Okay then, Ross, watch out!

She pushed open the bathroom door, walked in, and flung aside the shower curtain. "Want me to wash your back?"

Later, having managed—somehow—to resist Suzy in the shower, Kevin cinched the belt of his terry robe tightly around his waist and sat down and tried to read. Suzy settled happily at the far corner of the couch and slipped one bare foot onto his lap. She wiggled her toes, peeking at him over the edge of his newspaper. "Could you just rub my poor aching foot!" she asked sweetly, wiggling some more.

Begrudgingly, he drew his hand over her high, delicate arch. His fingers traced the curve of her heel, the faint blue veins at her ankle. Gently, and with great love, he began to massage her foot.

"Wonderful!" she whispered, sinking lower into the cushions. "And then my calf, and my thigh, and—"

He leaped from the sofa and headed for the closet and his clothes. "Let's go get some dinner."

"Fantastic. I'm starving too!" She grinned and dialed room service. She ordered rack of lamb for two, and a bottle of fine champagne. "Oh, and roses! I'll woo you with roses!" she said to Kevin happily, momentarily covering the receiver with her hand. "And what else? I know, caviar, and a gypsy violinist. . . . Uh-oh, cancel the violin. But send everything else, quick!"

The evening sent lengthening shadows trailing across the floor. Kevin and Suzy talked and laughed, but whenever Suzy would get just that little bit too close, Kevin would carefully open the distance between them. They both knew what was going on, but they were tired, tired from wanting and not having, and settled for this: the moment together, with the future waiting beyond the hotel room door.

Afterward, Kevin turned on the TV and Suzy snuggled warm against his side, her feet tucked up under her like a little girl. A short while later he nudged her awake.

"Look," he signed. "It's you. On TV. My Kevin's Kookie girl."

"Kevin's girl," she whispered in reply, and fell back asleep on his shoulder.

Slipping out from under her sweet, dear warmth, he went to stand at the window. A cool breeze blew in from the unseen ocean, and he crossed his arms over his aching chest and stared out into the night. Hours later, when Suzy stirred and called to him, he lifted her into his arms and carried her to the bed. Lying down beside her, he held her in his arms all night long, sleepless, staring into the dark.

A wake-up call roused Suzy to golden sunlight streaming in the window. It was morning and Kevin was gone again! There was only his note: *Dearest Suzy, Steve Kanasawa's wife said yes to Disneyland. I've arranged for a chauffeur to pick you up at 10:00. He has his instructions. I'll see you later. Love, Kevin.*

Oh, there were mysteries in that little note. How early had he gotten up? Had he kissed her before he left? Or stood and watched her sleep? And what did he mean by "he has his instructions"? Hmmm, there was a puzzle. And exactly when was "later"? How many hours, minutes, seconds till then? And "love"? Not "all my love," or "I'll love you forever" the way she would have signed a note to him. What *was* he plotting now, that man of hers?

Suzy dressed in minutes and was waiting beneath the canopied entrance when the chauffeur and Sandra Kanasawa arrived and whisked her off to Disneyland.

Sandra was delightful, eager, and curious, and she and Suzy hurried around all day like the wide-eyed tourists they were. When the sun began to dip behind the horizon, and Suzy realized the chauffeur would be there in minutes to pick them up, only her tired bones and the joyous thought of rushing back to the hotel and falling into Kevin's arms enticed her to leave the Magic Kingdom.

After dropping Sandra off at her apartment, the driver pulled the long, sleek limo into the frantic freeway traffic. Suzy leaned back against the buttery yellow leather and let her mind fill with thoughts of Kevin. Kevin, her stubborn prince, her knight in shining armor. Come what may, she loved that man. A warm rush of desire swept through her and she shivered slightly, then smiled to herself, closed her eyes, and dreamed lovely, private dreams as her chariot sped on through the L.A. traffic.

"Miss . . .?"

At first Suzy thought the light tapping was a bird, perhaps a snow-white dove flying out of a dream to greet her. She lifted one heavy eyelid slowly.

"Miss, we're here."

She raised the other lid and looked straight into the warm, round eyes of the chauffeur, who was leaning cautiously through the back door of the limousine. His mouth tilted into a grin. "M'drivin' was so smooth, you fell right asleep back here, ma'am."

She smiled hazily and covered her yawn with the back of one hand. "Yes, I did, didn't I?"

"I hated to wake you, miss, but we better hurry or you're sure to miss that plane back to K.C."

"Yes, you're prob—"

Suddenly Suzy lurched forward. Her eyes were open wide and all traces of sleep had vanished. "Plane? What are you talking about?" Her gaze searched the man's face, then she stared beyond him at the L.A. airport terminal. "Wh—"

The chauffeur grinned. "Mr. Ross said you might be a little surprised."

Suzy gritted her teeth. Surprised wasn't exactly the word for it! "But my things . . . ?"

She knew before the man spoke again what he was about to say. Oh, Kevin was so clever!

"They're all here, miss. Mr. Ross made sure of

that. And your ticket." He handed her the envelope proudly. "He said he took care of everything, that you weren't to worry about a thing. Nice man, that Mr. Ross."

She forced a smile into place as she stepped out of the limousine. "Yes, a lovely man." A lovely man who played rougher than she thought! Her mind whirling, Suzy stared at the chauffeur's back as he pulled her small suitcase out of the front seat. Well, we'll just see about this. Kevin Ross! He should know by now that there was nothing she liked better than a challenge! Smiling brightly now, she pressed a folded bill into the chauffeur's hand. "Thank you, sir."

"Thank *you*, ma'am." He nodded appreciatively, then pointed inside the car. "Say, don't forget that package you left there on the seat."

"Oh, thank you!" She smiled mysteriously. "I wouldn't want to forget that. It's a gift for a friend. A very *appropriate* gift!" She tucked one gray, floppy ear back inside the bulky Disneyland bag, shoved it under her arm, and strode resolutely into the airport.

Ten

"You'll be a good pair. Oh, yes, a *perfect* match!"

Suzy cradled the stuffed donkey in her arms and looked down at the big sad eyes. "Yes, Eeyore, you two should understand each other just fine." A tiny, mischievous grin tipped the edges of her mouth as she sprinted up the steps to the factory.

"Hello, Mike," she said as she stepped through the door and came face-to-face with the young lawyer.

"Suzy! What brings you over this way so early in the morning?" He eyed her warmups and tennis shoes. "New photo campaign twist—cookies while you trot?"

She laughed. "Nope. Just thought I'd bring Kevin a welcome-home present."

Mike looked down at the stuffed animal and lifted his brows. "Oh . . . I see."

She held up the donkey. "Eeyore, meet Mike. He's a good sort."

"Howdy, Eeyore, nice to meet you." He eyed the donkey carefully. "I have a sneaking suspicion that deep down, somewhere, there's a good reason for your being here."

"Yup, this is a smart man, Eeyore. A lawyer, you know."

"Unfortunately, Eeyore, even we lawywers can't always figure Suzy out."

Her light laughter floated through the hall. "I'm really very simple to understand, Mike."

He laughed. "Right! Too bad we can't say that about certain other folks. . . ."

"See, I knew you'd understand. And don't *you* think Kevin and he will be fine company?"

Mike's brows leaped up in amusement. "If you say so, Suzy. But I have a feeling I'd be better off not asking . . . or answering . . . any more questions."

"Silence is golden, right, Mike?" She winked and tossed the bright flame of her hair back off her face. She was glowing with mischief, and looking for more.

Mike bit back a grin and eyed her suspiciously. "Well, you probably ought to take Eeyore on in. The big man is in his office. That must have been *some* trip to California. He looks a bit under the weather: shadows under his eyes, his tie is crooked, and he hasn't cracked a joke all morning."

"Glad to hear that, Mike. I hope he's miserable!"

Mike shook his head and walked out the door laughing. Never a dull moment with Suzy around, he thought. Damned if she wasn't the best thing that ever happened to Kevin Ross. Maybe one of these days he'd even wake up and realize it!

Suzy waltzed down the hall and paused with her toes at Kevin's door. It was open a crack and she could see his body hunched over the desk, his head cradled in his arms. "Just like you, Eeyore," she whispered to the donkey in her arms. "He's busy feeling sorry for himself, shutting the world out. Well, I'll show him!"

She threw her shoulders back and marched into

the room. She slapped one hand down hard on the desk just in front of Kevin, making tiny flecks of dust dance in the morning light.

His head shot up and he stared at Suzy in disbelief. Damn, he thought. She'd gone from a fantasy in his mind to reality in his office, just like that! He shook his head, but Suzy didn't give him a minute to think.

She plopped the donkey down on the desk, its gray legs stretching out toward Kevin. "Here. I brought you a present. He's come all the way from my wonderful visit to Disneyland. Which, by the way, was lots of fun. Mickey Mouse seemed to appreciate my company." She paused for emphasis, then continued slowly so Kevin wouldn't miss a word. "Eeyore came to say good morning, if it *is* a good morning, which, as he wisely said, he doubts."

Kevin stared at the donkey, then looked up into Suzy's flashing eyes. "Suzy . . ."

She leaned over the desk until her face was just inches from his, her breath warm on his lips. The donkey was trapped in the narrow space between them, its furry legs digging into his chest. Then she leaned back so that Kevin easily could read her lips. "I thought you and Eeyore deserved each other. But let me set you straight on something, Kevin Ross. You can go ahead and act like an ass all you want . . ." Her eyes deepened to the green of the cool, deep sea and her mouth smiled sweetly. "*But* I am going to stick around anyway, because I know this is *real*. I love you, Kevin, and I'm going to get you!"

She was gone before Kevin could react. A flash of blue warmups and a heated stream of air were left in her wake.

Kevin shook his head as he stared at the empty doorway. His head was fuzzy from a chronic lack of sleep and he wondered for a brief moment if he'd imagined this latest encounter with Suzy Keller. But no, the pain in his heart told him she'd been here all right . . . that, and this damned donkey. He rubbed one hand across his face and stared for a long time at his new companion. "Eeyore, hmmm . . ." he said silently. "Well, buddy, do you play racquetball?"

"Man, you're vicious today!" Mike's words echoed off the walls and ceiling of the racquetball court as he wiped the perspiration from his forehead with the back of his hand.

Kevin leaned his dripping back against the wall and slid down until his knees met his chin. His chest heaved with exertion.

Mike walked over to his friend. "Suzy, huh?" he asked.

Kevin nodded.

"She's a great gal. And you're crazy about her. What's the problem?"

"*That's* exactly the problem!" Kevin signed angrily.

Mike shrugged. "Such problems I should have."

"Suzy's going to be someone someday."

"Good. And you already are, my friend. A perfect pair."

Kevin stared up at Mike, then shook his head. "It won't work, Mike. I'd be holding her back."

"From what?"

Kevin's hands lay limp for a moment. Why was Mike trying to make this sound simple? It sure as hell wasn't! Slowly, he tried to pull out the thoughts that were tangled up inside his head and heart. "I do love her, Mike. I love her so much, I want her to have everything. All her dreams."

"And Suzy's the kind who won't settle for less, Kevin. I agree."

"But dammit, Mike, the people she deals with, the social part—"

"You're going to the Chamber of Commerce luncheon tomorrow, right?" Mike interrupted abruptly.

Kevin nodded.

"Kevin, don't you see, you do that bit all the time! You were on national television—the *Today Show*!—for Pete's sake. Dinners, press conferences, cocktail parties. How much more public do you think Suzy will want to get? Besides, if you ask me, Suzy likes those deals about as much as you and I do. She'd much rather be out tackling you on a football field, or in your office, or wherever." He laughed. "Kevin, face it, you're pulling at straws."

Kevin's eyes were sad and faraway. "Okay. Maybe all that's true. But it's also true that I'm deaf, Mike. Dammit, I'm deaf!" The sign was heavy between them. "I love Suzy more than anything in this whole universe, and I can never, ever, give her a *normal* life."

"Maybe that just depends on your definition of normal." Mike looked down at his friend for a long time. There wasn't anything more he could say. No argument he could present that Kevin wouldn't counter. The anguish came from Kevin's heart. He'd have to find the answer there too.

Slowly, Kevin pulled himself up from the floor. And the two friends, each acutely aware of the other and of life's irrational twists, silently left the court.

Eleven

"Do I hear three kisses? Six kisses? An even dozen?" Suzy asked when Kevin picked her up that night. She tilted her lovely face up to receive his answer. "Come now, Mr. Ross, what am I bid for the pleasure of my company this evening?"

"The pleasure of your company is beyond price," he signed softly. Then he shoved his hands deep into his pockets and willed his body not to react.

Hopeless! he thought. He was hopeless! Hadn't he just told Mike how impossible this was? And now his muscles tensed with desire, his breath rasped in his throat. As though he had no will of his own, he circled his arms around her reed-slim body and kissed her soft, yielding mouth. He drew his lips softly across hers, savoring the sweetness of her, the brush of her hair against his cheek, the press of her breasts against his chest. With a groan he pulled away and leaned back against the wall outside her door.

"Ummm . . . that was nice," she said, "but it was only one. One kiss? Is that all I'm bid?" Smoothing her hands down the pale chiffon skirt of her cocktail dress, she frowned. "Goodness, if that's any indication of how I'm going to do this evening, the Rotary Club had better find a new auctioneer."

"The Rotary Club had better not be auctioning off your kisses!" Kevin's hands snapped the air.

"Oh, good! Just the answer I was hoping for. I *do* love you, Mr. Ross." She slipped a hand into the crook of his arm and let her fingers rest against the warm skin of his forearm. He was wearing a white business shirt, the sleeves rolled back to his elbows, the crispness surrendering to a long, hard day at the warehouse. He looked rumpled and sexy. She adored him. "And the answer is 'no.' They're auctioning off the one hundred dozen cookies you donated, and everything else it seems, from roller skates to a week on the French Riviera. Nice place for a honeymoon, or so I've heard."

He steered her quickly down the hall, into the elevator, and out the front door. "You'll be late," he signed. "We wouldn't want the entire Rotary Club angry with you."

"Hey," she cried, digging in her heels. "Where's the van, my wonderful Kevin's Kookies van with my picture on it?"

"I borrowed Mike's car. He wasn't needing it, and I thought I'd at least get you there in style."

"I like *your* style!" she retorted, settling with a pout into Mike Pepper's little black sports car. Kevin slammed her door shut, then climbed into the driver's seat and banged his head on the sunroof. "Just have to adjust the seat," he signed, scowling, and slammed his knees into the dash. He muttered a quick, clipped curse.

Suzy hid her laughter behind her hands. When she could keep a straight face, she scolded, "There, you did it again. Wasting your breath on a silly obscenity when you could be saying something really worthwhile. Like my name. Or 'I love you.'

Now *that* would be worth speaking aloud for, my darling."

He didn't respond. When he slid to a stop in front of the hotel, he signed, "Here we are. Have fun. Raise lots of money for those little kids, and . . . Well, just have a good time."

"Won't you come with me? There's a dinner-dance after—"

"I'm not dressed for it."

"So I noticed. But you did that on purpose, knowing I'd make you get up and dance with me, and smile at the cameras, and you'd have to let down that shield of yours."

"It's nothing like that," he lied, avoiding her bright gaze. "It was just a busy day. And there have been some problems at the factory. Really," he insisted, and climbed out from behind the wheel. He waved away the doorman and opened Suzy's door. "You look beautiful. They'll love you."

"Everyone who matters already does," she said, and squeezed his hand.

She sashayed away, the pale petals of chiffon floating down over her hips and calves. The straps of her evening sandals criss-crossed that slender foot he had once held in his hand. He could feel the shape of it now, burned into his palm. The shape and texture of her whole body were burned into his flesh, into his very soul. The ache of wanting her, loving her, was so strong, it made him lean back against the sleek low hood of the car.

Just then Suzy turned, her smile bright and confident. She waved, and then was gone.

Kevin stood there for a moment staring at the space where she'd stood, still seeing her there. So, now it's mirages, Ross, he thought. What's next? The question of the hour . . . What's next? This crazy dance he was doing had to come to an end soon. Two steps forward, one step back . . . and then where? He took a ragged breath and slipped back into the car.

As Kevin drove to the warehouse, he wished the moon wouldn't shine, the breeze wouldn't blow, the stars would vanish and leave the night sky as empty and lonely as he suddenly felt. He wished it would rain, hail, sleet . . . turn into a blinding snowstorm that would take his mind off everything but the road ahead. Swallowing around the raw ache in his throat, he tightened his grip on the wheel. Right now, the road ahead looked mighty empty and lonely.

The square, squat shape of the factory was a welcome sight. Business, he thought. And business problems. *That* he could handle. Someone had been stealing cartons of cookies, just a few at a time, petty stuff and hardly worth the effort. But it had to be one of his people, and that was what worried Kevin. Who and why? And then there was the boy, Vinnie, the same boy he had saved from being crushed by the truck that first Saturday Suzy had come to work. That first day . . . It seemed like years ago, or just a heartbeat before. . . .

Shaking his head, he corralled his thoughts back to business. Vinnie had been unreliable lately, picking arguments with the other workers, showing up late or not at all. Was there some tie-in? Well, he'd hang around tonight and see.

Kevin parked the little sports car safely off the street near the loading dock and let himself in the side door. He took one step inside and froze. There was a light on in the men's room at the far end of the warehouse. The janitor? The foreman working late? Or maybe just a light left on by accident. Some sixth sense told him it was none of those things. Someone was in there. Someone who hadn't expected him back tonight. Who?

In absolute silence he wound his way through the dark warehouse toward the knife-thin slice of light showing under the door. He placed his hand flat against the door itself, drew a deep, muscle-tensing breath, and pushed it slowly open.

Vinnie was standing there, hunched over the sink, sprinkling white powder from a little vial onto a paper towel. Kevin took in the whole scene in about a second and a half, and exploded into the room.

"Dammit, don't you touch that crap!" He knocked the kid back against the tile wall and signed right in his face, his hands slashing angrily through the air. "Are you crazy? Don't you have enough problems without looking for more?"

"Leave me alone, damn you!" the kid shouted back, his signs just as angry. "Problems? My whole damn life is nothing but problems, and you're one of them! Yeah, you, the big boss. Superman. Everyone's hero." Vinnie's signs faltered, stopped, and he turned around and slammed his forehead against the tile.

Kevin pulled him back against him and the boy pushed his wet face against his shoulder.

Kevin laid a hand softly on the boy's fair head and let him cry. "Hey," he signed later. "Hey . . . it's okay. It'll all be all right. Just talk to me, Vinnie, okay?"

"I—I just can't stand it sometimes," the boy signed, wiping his eyes with the back of one hand. "I try, really I do. And nothing seems to work."

"I know," Kevin signed softly.

"No! You can't! *You* can do anything. You're the best, the greatest. And I want to be like you, but I just can't do anything right. I'm always on the outside looking in, and when I try to be like everyone else, they look at me like I'm invisible, like I don't even exist!"

"Oh, God, I remember. . . ."

"No—"

"Yes. Believe me." And he did. He had been that boy, with all the same pain, the frustration, and embarrassment. The wanting and never getting, until you were afraid to hope, afraid to try, afraid to get hurt again. He shook his head. "But if you don't try, you'll never have *anything*, Vinnie. You'll never be all you can be. You'll settle for less, and spend your whole life regretting it. Sure, it takes courage. More courage than you think you've got sometimes. And patience. And determination. You can't be just as good as everyone else, you've got to be better! You've got to be the best. Always. You've got to work harder, think faster, give more of yourself."

"But I try. And I get slapped in the face."

"Then you've got to turn the other cheek. And then you go on from there. But you've got to know you have friends who love you, people who care . . . who respect and support you. Nobody can do it alone."

"*You* do!"

"Hell, no! I've got good friends all around me. And you guys, all of you here. I count on you, trust you. I'm strong because you are. And I have a wonderful woman who loves me—"

The words were out before he knew they were there. But it was the truth, wasn't it, Ross? he asked himself. The most wonderful woman in the world loved him, and he'd never have to go it alone . . . never. Happiness, like a wild, dark wing, beat at his heart. The joy of it spilled onto his face in a smile.

"Did I say something funny?" Vinnie asked, puzzled.

"No. I was just thinking about love."

"Heck, I know what you mean! See, that's what

started all this. I was dating Louise, you know, with the ponytail—"

"I know. Pretty girl."

"You bet. And I thought, well . . . I thought I'd go apply for a job I saw in the paper. Assistant foreman of a warehouse over in Lenexa . . . Not that I'm not happy here," he added quickly. "But I thought it would be a real step up, and I could buy her a ring and she'd be proud of me—" His signs fizzled in a wave of misery. "Hell, they didn't think I could sweep the floor."

"But you could. And you could be a damn good assistant foreman if that's what you wanted."

"Damn right!"

"Then you've got to prove it by taking everything that life dishes out and keeping your courage, your self-respect, your pride. But, Vinnie—" Kevin stopped and stabbed one blunt finger at the white powder on the paper towel. "That is not the answer. That's the answer to *nothing*. It's the easy way to nowhere."

"Yeah . . . but it helps block it out—"

"Only temporarily, Vinnie."

Vinnie looked at Kevin for a long moment. Then, his shoulders slumped, he slowly shook the towel into the sink. He turned the faucet on and stared into the swirling water. "But sometimes I just get scared."

"So come to me then. I haven't got all the answers, but I've been down the same road. You might as well use my experience. That's the point, kid. Use what you've got: ambition, brains, a good family, an education. Next time we'll run through a practice interview so you'll know what to expect, and how to cope with it. And you need a decent résumé, so people can see what you've done, what you can do . . . and not just that you're deaf. Hell, everyone's got some weak spot, but you can't use deafness as an excuse for not going after what you want."

Hey, Ross, he thought, grinning wryly, do you know what you just said? "You can't use deafness as an excuse. . . ." Well, mister, welcome to the future!

He and Vinnie spent the rest of the night talking. Kevin did his share of lecturing, while Vinnie packed cartons, loaded the van, and cleaned the entire warehouse until it sparkled. "Consider this overtime to pay for my missing cookies," Kevin told him. "And it better not happen again."

"Never!" Vinnie promised. "Heck, I wouldn't dare. You know everything."

"Not everything, kid." He grinned. "But I'm making strides."

At dawn they locked the place up. Vinnie caught the bus home and Kevin slipped into Mike's car. In minutes he was racing down the interstate to Mike's Johnson County condo. He knocked on the door, waited two minutes, and knocked again, louder.

"Okay, I'm comin', I'm comin'!" Mike grumbled, stumbling out of the bedroom, one leg in his pajama bottoms.

Kevin knocked a third time, even more insistently.

"Hold your horses!" an irate Mike yelled, and yanked the door open. "Kevin!" He groaned. "Dammit, man, it's six o'clock in the morning."

"I know. Sorry, I didn't mean to wake you up."

"Well." Mike pulled his friend inside and lowered his voice. "You didn't exactly wake me up. I was . . . well, celebrating the dawn with a lady friend."

"I really *am* sorry, pal!" Kevin sighed, his dark

brows meeting over his even darker eyes. Impatience gnawed at him like a dog worrying a bone, but he forced a shrug. "Listen, I'll come back later—"

"Hell, you don't look like you'll last till later. What's up?"

"I'm in love."

"*Great.* Break in here at six o'clock in the morning to tell me something I already know. The whole world knows! That's *great,* Ross!"

"Sorry again." Kevin grinned. "But it just sort of hit me last night, what that really means, buddy. I love that woman! And she loves me! And we're going to spend our whole wonderful lives together!"

Mike caught Kevin's grin and flashed it back. "That is great news, Kevin, and I'm happy for you both. But don't you think you should be telling *her* all this. When I saw her last night at the auction, she said you were still playing hard to get."

"I know. I must have been crazy."

"Temporary insanity, I agree."

"But I've got something to do first. And you're going to help me. I've got to go talk to her parents."

"Don't you think that's carrying chivalry too far nowadays? Asking for her hand—"

"I'm not asking. I'm telling. But I want a chance to explain how much I love her, and why this is worth all the risk!"

Mike put his hands on his friend's shoulders. "Kevin. There's no risk for you two. Just happiness."

Kevin swallowed hard. "Thanks, Mike. But I need you to help me tell them that. Okay?"

"Sure!" Mike grinned and grabbed Kevin in a big bear hug.

•　•　•

The sun played peek-a-boo with the clouds as Mike and Kevin drove up Ward Parkway. Light reigned, then shadow, chasing each other across the landscaped lawns and fountains, making rainbows appear in the spray, then just as quickly vanish.

Kevin's mood shifted as wildly. There was a fire raging in his loins, a cold chill climbing his spine. Maybe he should just tell Mike to turn this thing around and take him right to Suzy's, he thought. Maybe this was a mistake. Was he being realistic before or just stubborn? Was he right now, or just plain crazy with love? What would her parents think of his showing up on their doorstep at dawn, fully equipped with an interpreter? If they objected, would it hurt Suzy more than his never having tried to talk to them? But at least he'd try. He loved her so much, he wanted everyone she loved to be happy with them. Surely no one could be this happy and be wrong! Or . . . could they?

"Mike, I love this woman." His signs jumped with the tension burning through his veins.

"Relax, partner. This is gonna be a piece of cake."

Kevin groaned and raked his fingers through his hair.

There wasn't a sign of life at the Keller home. The shades were still drawn, the newspaper was lying in wait on the doorstep. Mike swung into the wide, curved driveway and parked. "This is the place, right?"

Kevin glanced bleakly at the address and nodded.

"Well, then, how about it?"

"How about a beer instead?" he parried. He rolled his shoulders to ease the tension that had knotted there, digging its fingers into the base of his skull.

"At eight A.M.?"

"Right! Let's go." He climbed out of the car, strode up to the door, and knocked. He waited one minute, then raised his arm to knock again, louder.

Mike restrained him, grinning. "Easy, Kevin! These folks may not be as glad to see you as I was."

Kevin shoved his hands into his pockets, glowering at that dark, nerve-shattering thought. And that was what Bea Keller saw when she opened the door in her robe.

"Why, Kevin! What a nice surprise!" she said with a smile, her hand flying to her sleep-mussed hair. "And Mr. Pepper, isn't it? We met at the cocktail party . . . ."

"Mike, please, Mrs. Keller."

"Then it's Bea here. Well, what a nice surprise. . . . Won't you both come in? Charles! Oh, Charles, we have company," she called, leading the way into the sunlit breakfast nook.

"Company?" her husband echoed in dismay, but his confusion changed to a broad smile as they entered the room. "Well, Kevin! It's good to see you. And Mike Pepper, corporate lawyer extraordinaire, right?"

"The dynamic duo at your service!" Kevin joked, signing as Mike translated.

"Well, you certainly looked the hero on that TV show, Kevin. We were very proud of you."

"Thank you, sir. I appreciate that."

"Coffee?" Bea asked, catching her husband's eye in a puzzled glance over the young men's heads as she poured. Charles nodded.

"So," Charles said, "what brings you two out so early this morning? No problem, I hope. . . ."

Kevin set his cup down and squared his broad shoulders. If they had known him better, the Kellers would have seen the flash of desperation in his dark eyes. Lord, he thought, he'd faced tougher situations than this without flinching. He'd overcome greater obstacles, fought greater odds. He was tough, strong, confident, and assured. Then why was his heart hammering against his ribs, the sweat gathering under his arms? Dammit all, Ross, he told himself. This is no time to panic. They think you're a hero. Go with it! He nodded at Mike and started to sign.

"Mr. Keller . . . Charles, Bea. You must know that I love Suzy." He swallowed, a frown shadowing his eyes as he looked from one to the other. "I love her very much. With all my heart and soul. And I want to marry her." He halted, watching the emotions chase across their faces as they listened to Mike's voice speaking his words. If he was looking for clues, he got none, and had to plunge on defenseless. "I'm going to ask Suzy to marry me. But first I wanted us to have a chance to talk. I'm sure you must have questions, concerns . . . and I wanted us to be honest with each other. Please. Tell me. What do you think of our relationship? How do you feel about your daughter being in love with a deaf man?"

Charles and Bea Keller looked at each other, then at the honest young man sitting across the breakfast table from them, and they smiled. Bea nodded, and Charles spoke for them both.

"Son, I'll tell you. We've talked this over, of course, and we think it all comes down to this: We weren't ready for Suzy to fall in love. It didn't seem to fit in the old game plan, you see. Nope, we weren't ready at all. But maybe parents never are. And you, Kevin, well, you sure did take us by surprise. But since she loves you as much as you obviously love her, and since you are the reason she's so very happy now, well, we're all for it!"

Kevin wanted to throw back his head and whoop

with joy. He wanted to leap across the table and hug them both. He wanted to take Suzy in his arms and hold her forever. Instead, he clenched and unclenched his hands, let out the breath he hadn't even known he was holding, and looked earnestly at his future in-laws. "I *will* make her happy. You can trust me on that! But aren't there any questions? Worries?"

"Oh, we had plenty of those," Charles said. "But we've watched you, watched Suzy. We've seen her joy *because* of you."

His wife interrupted, slipping from her chair and facing Kevin with both hands planted on her hips. "*My* only worry," she scolded, "is that you are not going to smile for the wedding pictures! And then I would be quite furious!"

"No problem," he answered, relaxing into a grin that would have melted their hearts if he hadn't already won them.

"Hey, now *there's* cause for celebration," Mike said, jabbing Kevin in the ribs. "And you better keep practicing. You've got that Chamber of Commerce luncheon to attend in about three hours."

"Luncheon, hell! I'm going to find Suzy—"

"You'll find her right there!" Mike promised.

"And you don't want to miss *this* luncheon. Suzy said—" Charles began, then caught his wife's warning look.

"What? What did Suzy say?" Kevin asked, narrowing his eyes. Something was going on here. . . .

But no one seemed interested in talking about it anymore.

The Chamber of Commerce luncheon was held in the new Vista Hotel, and Suzy felt as new and elegant as the meeting room as she circulated among the small groups after the luncheon. She didn't know when the fears had evaporated entirely or her heart had completely opened. All she knew was that everything was right and exactly the way it should be—or at least would be soon!

Shortly before the mayor had presented Kevin with the coveted Man of the Year award, asserting that Kevin was "certainly an outstanding example for young people venturing into business." They'd all basked in the warmth of Kevin's honor. Everyone— Susan, Logan, Mike, her parents—they'd all come, all applauded joyously, all felt so inextricably wound up in this wonderful man and what he'd done.

And the Kevin's Kookies campaign *was* a success. A spectacular success from all reports. Just as it should be! Just as her *own* secret campaign would be. And there was no time to start it like the present!

She grinned to herself and shook the hand of a society matron, smiling brightly as she chatted about cookies and campaigns . . . and Kevin Ross.

Across the room Kevin nodded, smiled, and politely accepted the continuous compliments coming his way. The Chamber's Man of the Year award had been a surprise. Lately he'd been much too busy to think of things like that. But the honor had stirred him in a way public acclaim usually didn't. He felt good, very good. And the secret in his heart made him feel even better.

Immediately, his gaze shifted beyond the whitehaired man shaking his hand and lighted on Suzy. Amazing how that happened, he mused. He could look up from anywhere, in any direction, and Suzy seemed to fill his sight. Lovely, smiling, seductive Suzy, whose presence filled his whole being. Even when he had been struggling to put some physical distance between them, it had been absolutely impossible to keep her out of his thoughts and dreams. She possessed him completely.

The thought made him feel incredibly happy. And incredibly aroused. Oh, Suzy. . . . He sighed, wanting her. He wanted to feel the warmth of her gaze on his face, the sweetness of her in his arms. But they hadn't had a second alone together since he set foot in the hotel. Hell, she didn't even know what he was thinking.

Or did she?

She had a glow about her, her emerald eyes sparkling jewel-bright, that spoke of some secret *she* knew. And that smile, that bright, teasing, loving smile flashed at him across the crowded room and made his heart stop beating.

Suzy laughed softly, feeling the force of Kevin's gaze. She chatted effusively with everyone who came her way, reporters, friends, Chamber members. They seemed to hang on her words, and as she walked away from them their gazes followed her happily.

The pumping on his hand drew Kevin's focus back to the couple standing in front of him.

"Marvelous, Mr. Ross, simply wonderful!" the middle-aged woman gushed. "We're all so happy. My, the event of the year!"

Kevin smiled.

"Yes, sir," her husband continued. "A perfect match-up from all sides!"

A younger woman, whom Kevin remembered meeting at a press conference earlier, joined them. "Mr. Ross, this is, without a doubt, the most exciting Chamber luncheon I've ever attended! We're all thrilled for you! Such wonderful news!" She pulled out a pad of paper. "Now, I want *every* detail!"

Kevin looked at her closely, wondering what he'd missed. But before he had a chance to ask, his attention was captured by Susan and Logan's son Daniel, who rushed to his side and hung tightly to his arm. *His* family, Kevin had always called them, and today they were all here to celebrate. Daniel's upturned face was wreathed in grins and chocolate cake. "Nice goin', unc! Cool!"

Kevin grinned. "So, little buddy, you approve of the award?" he signed carefully.

Daniel looked puzzled for a moment, then understanding washed across his face. "Oh, that! Yeah, great, Uncle Kevin! But I meant—"

"Hey, you stinker, you!" Logan came up just then and slapped Kevin forcefully on the back. "Fantastic news! This has turned into quite a day, my friend. Susan's beside herself!"

Logan started to say more, but the mayor arrived and hustled a confused Kevin off to have his picture taken with him.

Something was going on, Kevin thought, that everyone seemed to know about, everyone but *him*, the guest of honor! What had he missed? He searched his mind, going carefully over the speeches that were given, the comments made before the award was presented. No, nothing made any sense.

"Hey, Kevin, smile, like *happy*, you know!" the young photographer said, grinning. "Save those expressions for the big day. *That's* when you should look worried and confused." He laughed, then snapped the picture.

Kevin escaped as soon as he could and looked around for Mike. Mike would explain why everyone was acting . . . well, so peculiar. Sometimes this happened, Kevin knew. Sometimes he *did* miss something and Mike could set him straight in an instant. That was all it was, some little thing he missed. . . .

"Kevin!" Susan's arms were around him, crushing him to her. When she finally pulled away, Kevin saw there were tears in her eyes.

"Susan, are you all right?" he signed quickly.

"Oh, Kevin," she said slowly and lovingly. "You should have known I'd cry. You deserve happiness. And I'm just so very, very glad for you." The tears slid down her cheeks and she hugged him again.

Now, wait a minute! He hadn't said anything, and certainly *she* couldn't read his mind too. Frowning, he held her away and studied her face. Then he signed, "Susan, this is a nice award. But tears?"

"Kevin, stop it!" She caught his hands in hers and scowled at him. "You know that's not what I mean. The award is terrific. But that I've had time to digest. It's Suzy."

"Suzy?" Kevin's heart stopped beating. It had happened, he thought. She'd been stolen away by some powerful offer: a movie or *Vogue* or New York or Europe. . . . His mind was spinning. He had known it would happen; he had told her so himself! But so soon? Now? No, he couldn't bear for her to leave him now. No! And Susan *wouldn't* be happy. She knew how he felt. Surely she knew this would kill him.

"Susan," he signed abruptly, "tell me! What the hell are you talking about?"

Startled, Susan stared up at him, then looked around at the others, who were approaching them with the same delighted expressions on their faces. She reached up and touched his cheek, then shook her head. "Oh, dear, dear Kevin, it's not a secret anymore. I'm talking about Suzy's announcement."

Kevin took a quick, deep breath of cool air, knowing instinctively he was going to need it badly.

"About your engagement. You and Suzy! It's absolutely wonderful!"

Twelve

Heart pounding, Suzy lifted her head and peeked across the heads of the crowd milling around the ballroom.

Uh-oh! she thought. There he was, coming straight at her, his long strides gobbling up the width of the room, and he was *not* smiling.

"Kevin, I—"

He stopped right in front of her, planted his hands square on his hips, and looked deep into her eyes. His own dark eyes were flashing, and for once she couldn't read what was in their depths.

"Suzy—"

"The cat's out of the bag?" she asked, making it sound like a question she didn't want to hear the answer to.

"Whiskers and all!" he signed back. "Suzy, why—"

She cut him off, unable to stop the words that leaped from her heart. "Because I love you, Kevin Ross. And the loving are the daring!"

The room grew silent.

"Come with me," he signed, holding out his hand. Only his steady gaze kept her from fainting dead away in front of everyone, but she shook her head.

"I think I'd better stay right here. Safety in numbers and all that." She laughed nervously, jamming both hands into her pockets.

"Come with me, Suzy?" he asked, his hand out, waiting. "Love, come home with me?"

Suddenly his eyes, his soul were open to her.

Trembling, she put her hand in his.

With a hurried good-bye, they dashed from the room, down the wide staircase, and out the doors, leaving people standing open-mouthed and wondering in their wake. Suzy held tight to the cool strength of his hand and ran, laughing and crying at the same time. "You know what?" she said, stopping finally to catch her breath. "I wouldn't turn back now even if I lost my glass slipper."

"And I wouldn't let you," he answered, stopping beside her and smiling down into her lovely face. "I'd take you barefoot. Barefoot and beautiful. Forever." He folded her in his arms and held her close, so close that she could feel the pounding of his heart, the rapid rise and fall of his chest.

"I like that word," she said, leaning back to look at him.

"I like it, too, Suzy. Will you marry me?"

For an answer she planted a kiss on his lips, then another and another.

He cupped her face in his hands and covered her with kisses, hungry loving little souvenirs of yesterday's passion, little promises for tomorrow.

There was a titter of high childish laughter. Suzy pulled away slightly, and the two of them found themselves surrounded by an audience of children, baseballs and jump ropes and books in hand, all suddenly in no hurry to get on home from school.

Blushing and laughing, Suzy and Kevin shooed

them on, then leaned against each other, arms twined around each other's waists. Suddenly he released her, tipped her chin up with one finger, and signed, "I think we'd better get on home before I lose all self-control and get us arrested." His eyes had darkened to a coal-black smolder.

"Yes. Oh, yes. It would be a shame to spend our honeymoon in jail, when I was the highest bidder for that wonderful week on the French Riviera."

"You what?" That same dark brow swooped up into his hair, but she was getting used to it now and it only lifted a smile to her lips.

"Uh-oh. Have I done it again?" she teased. Reaching up, she pressed her lips to that wayward brow.

He tucked her hair behind one ear and drew the backs of his fingers tenderly down her cheek. "Any more surprises I need to know about?"

"Dozens. Hundreds! But you don't get to see a single one till we're home. Alone—just—the—two—of—us. A glass of wine. Some candlelight. Your bed."

Kevin hailed a cab and in minutes they were home. He opened the door and they stepped inside, and already it was different. Her favorite paintings were on the wall, her plants on his windowsill, her clothes in the closet, her toothbrush next to his. He felt like a stranger suddenly, newly arrived in this place. He looked over at her and she smiled.

"I know," she said, reading his mind as she did so often, he wasn't even surprised. "I feel like I've never been here before." She laughed, rubbing her hands up and down her arms. "But then, I feel like I've never been *anywhere* before. I'm even all new inside my skin. Brand new. Coming alive for the very first time. Want to see?"

Without waiting for an answer, she began to take off her clothes, piece by piece. She folded her suit jacket, her blouse, her skirt across the back of the couch. Then she paused for a moment, not hesitating, but giving him time to catch his breath.

He couldn't. It was as if his body had forgotten everything but how to want her, how to love her. Stepping close, he urged the strap of her slip down over the golden curve of her shoulder. Then the other strap. He slid his hands down her lovely silken body, tugging the slip completely off. She stepped out of the small circle of fabric and into the waiting circle of his arms.

With a groan of pure arousal, he lifted her in his arms and carried her to the bed. He laid her down on the quilt and stood there, his eyes devouring her, his broad chest rising and falling heavily. Smiling, she reached up and laid a hand on his belt buckle. In a minute, maybe less, he was out of his clothes and stretched, naked and yearning, alongside her. His bronze skin was glazed with a sheen of sweat, but still he waited, holding his passion on a tight rein.

"Suzy, are you sure?"

"Yes. I'm sure."

"But you do realize what it means? My being deaf?"

"I know it means you'll never hear me say the words, 'I love you, Kevin Ross,' but I'll tell you anyway . . . so many ways. I know it means you'll never hear the racing of my heart when I'm close to you like this, loving you, wanting you. But you can feel it. Here . . ." She put his hand under her breast and pressed it to her skin. "Feel it?"

"Yes." He slid his hand up over the lovely fullness of her breast until her nipple nestled in his palm.

It was a gesture so loving, so tender, that it brought tears to her eyes.

She drew her fingertips slowly, gently, across

his chest, over his ribs, as her thoughts struggled to take shape in words. Then she lifted her hand and placed its comforting warmth against his cheek. "I know it means you'll never hear our babies cry, or say their first words . . . or their second or third. And I know that will be hard. That will make you sad, and I'll share your sadness, Kevin. But I'll also share your happiness when they roll over for the first time, or take their first steps, or ride a bike. And for every sadness, there will be a hundred happinesses, darling. In that, we're no different from anyone else. For us all, there's happiness and sadness all mixed together, but that, my love, is life. And that's what I want to share with you. My life. Forever."

"Suzy. I love you."

He said it out loud, a soft, husky whisper full of love and trust and belief in happily-ever-after.

"Oh, Kevin, Kevin . . ."

Then his hands were threading through her hair, cupping her head, tilting her face up to his, and she was pressing against him, wrapping her arms tight around his neck, and crying, kissing him and being kissed back with a sweetness that left them both breathless and trembling.

"One more thing!" she said as she pulled away ever so slightly. "I guess I'll just have to get used to making love with the lights on so that we can talk."

A sudden spark of mischief flashed in his eyes. "Let's turn them off and see what happens."

Getting out of bed, he strode around the room, naked and gleaming, his muscles moving beneath his tanned skin across his shoulders, back, buttocks, thighs. He pulled each shade, then returned to her. He wrapped his legs around hers and pulled her close. The room was bathed in darkness, with just a golden haze filtering in around the shades.

Suzy giggled, quivering with anticipation and pleasure. A low, husky laugh rumbled in Kevin's throat.

He brushed the flat of his hand across her belly as if erasing a board. Then, using his index finger, he wrote the words: "I love you."

"I love you too," she traced across his chest.

"For always."

"And ever."

"Well. What do you think? Will this work?"

He could feel her laughing again, shaking her head. She drew a big question mark across his chest, dropping the dot at the bottom into his belly button.

His laughter mingled with hers, and the bed began to shake. "I said, do you think this will work?"

Laughing, she rolled on top of him, straddling him and letting her hair spill across his face. Reaching up, she flicked the lamp by the bed on. There were two spots of color high on her cheeks and her eyes were shining. Talking through the giggles that shook her pale shoulders and breasts, she asked, "What?"

"I said, I think we need some practice."

"Oh, yes. Truly. We must do this more often."

"How often?" he asked, and caressed her arms, her back, her silken thighs.

"Daily. Twice daily. Every single minute!"

"Why, Suzy Keller. What's gotten into you?"

"Love," she said. "I told you, the loving are the daring. And that's us. Together."

THE EDITOR'S CORNER

Home for the Holidays! Certainly home is the nicest place to be in this upcoming season . . . and coming home, finding a home, perfecting one are key elements in each of our LOVESWEPTs next month.

First, in Peggy Webb's delightful **SCAMP OF SALTILLO,** LOVESWEPT #170, the heroine is setting up a new home in a small Mississippi town. Kate Midland is a witty, lovely, committed woman whose determination to save a magnolia tree imperiled by a construction crew brings her into face-to-face confrontation with Saltillo's mayor, Ben Adams. What a confrontation! What a mayor! Ben is self-confident, sensual, funny, generous . . . and perfect for Kate. But it takes a wacky mayoral race—including goats, bicycles, and kisses behind the bandstand—to bring these two fabulous people together. A romance with real heart and humor!

It is their homes—adjacent apartments—that bring together the heroine and hero in **FINNEGAN'S HIDEAWAY,** LOVESWEPT #171, by talented Sara Orwig. Lucy Reardon isn't really accident prone, but try to convince Finn Mundy of that. From the moment he spots the delectable-looking Lucy, her long, long shapely legs in black net stockings, he is falling . . . for her, with her, even

(continued)

off a ladder on top of her! But what are a few bruises, a minor broken arm compared to the enchantment and understanding Lucy offers? When Finn's brothers—and even his mother—show up on the doorstep, the scene is set for some even wilder misunderstandings and mishaps as Finn valiantly tries to handle that mob, his growing love for Lucy, law school exams, and his failing men's clothing business. A real charmer of a love story!

In the vivid, richly emotional **INHERITED,** LOVESWEPT #172, by gifted Marianne Shock, home is the source of a great deal of the conflict between heroine Tricia Riley and hero Chase Colby. Tricia's father hires Texas cowboy Chase to run Tricia's Virginia cattle ranch. Their attraction is instantaneous, explosive . . . as powerful as their apprehensions about sharing the running of the ranch. He brings her the gift of physical affection, for she was a child who lost her mother early in life and had never known her father's embrace or sweet words. She gives Chase the gift of emotional freedom and, at last, he can confide feelings he's never shared. But before these two ardent, needy people can come together both must deal with their troublesome pasts. A love story you'll cherish!

In **EMERALD FIRE,** LOVESWEPT #173, that marvelous storyteller Nancy Holder gives us a delightful couple in Stacy Livingston and Keith

(continued)

Mactavish . . . a man and a woman who seem worlds apart but couldn't be more alike at heart. And how does "home" play a part here? For both Stacy and Keith home means roots—his are in the exotic land of Hawaii, where ancestors and ancient gods are part of everyday life. Stacy has never felt she had any real roots, and has tried to find them in her work toward a degree as a marine biologist. Keith opens his arms and his home to her, sharing his large and loving family, his perceptions of sensual beauty and the real romance of life. You'll relish this exciting and provocative romance!

Home for the Holidays . . . in every heartwarming LOVESWEPT romance next month. Enjoy. And have a wonderful Thanksgiving celebration in your home!

Warm wishes,

Carolyn Nichols

Carolyn Nichols
  Editor
LOVESWEPT
Bantam Books, Inc.
666 Fifth Avenue
New York, NY 10103

His love for her is madness.
Her love for him is sin.

Sunshine
and
Shadow

by Sharon and Tom Curtis

COULD THEIR EXPLOSIVE LOVE BRIDGE THE CHASM BETWEEN TWO IMPOSSIBLY DIFFERENT WORLDS?

He thought there were no surprises left in the world ... but the sudden appearance of young Amish widow Susan Peachey was astonishing—and just the shock cynical Alan Wilde needed. She was a woman from another time, innocent, yet wise in ways he scarcely understood.

Irresistibly, Susan and Alan were drawn together to explore their wildly exotic differences. And soon they would discover something far greater—a rich emotional bond that transcended both of their worlds and linked them heart-to-heart ... until their need for each other became so overwhelming that there was no turning back. But would Susan have to sacrifice all she cherished for the uncertain joy of their forbidden love?

"Look for full details on how to win an authentic Amish quilt displaying the traditional 'Sunshine and Shadow' pattern in copies of SUNSHINE AND SHADOW or on displays at participating stores. No purchase necessary. Void where prohibited by law. Sweepstakes ends December 15, 1986."

Look for SUNSHINE AND SHADOW in your bookstore or use this coupon for ordering: